T. H. ELKMAN

A WESTERN NOVEL

ERIC H. HEISNER

Illustrations by Al P. Bringas

SKYHORSE PUBLISHING

Skyhorse Publishing books may be purchased in bulk at special discounts for sales promotion, corporate gifts, fund-raising, or educational purposes. Special editions can also be created to specifications. For details, contact the Special Sales Department, Skyhorse Publishing, 307 West 36th Street, 11th Floor, New York, NY 10018 or info@skyhorse-publishing.com.

Skyhorse® and Skyhorse Publishing® are registered trademarks of Skyhorse Publishing, Inc.®, a Delaware corporation.

Visit our website at www.skyhorsepublishing.com.

10 9 8 7 6 5 4 3 2 1

Library of Congress Cataloging-in-Publication Data is available on file.

Cover design by Tom Lau
Cover photo credit: iStock

Print ISBN: 978-1-5107-1186-0
Ebook ISBN: 978-1-5107-1187-7

Printed in the United States of America

Dedication

To my wife & children who fuel my passion.

Special Thanks

Al P. Bringas, Amber W. Heisner, Mark Bedor, Ron & Lori Heisner, Tim & Suzie Word, Clint & Billie Beach.

A very special thanks to: Dan Farnam who captures the visuals of my imagination through motion pictures and stills, Kimberley Lim and the experienced staff at Skyhorse Publishing, and my deepest gratitude to the Kishwaukee Valley Vigilance Committee for their unending source of rich characters.

The American West: A place where men find themselves through harsh and cruel circumstances and lives are short lived. Where women are as hard as the steel of a gun and the sweet burn of whiskey eases the rough, ratted edges. A life where death is a pill that must be swallowed and senses are developed beyond true human comprehension.

Introduction

I have always enjoyed tales of the Old West. As a storyteller, my writings in the Western genre have been about men of action and the consequences of their choices. This is my second novel following the release of *West to Bravo*, a John Wayne/John Ford–styled high-adventure, action piece. Bringing a new set of characters to life, the story of T. H. Elkman is a slice of life and a journey that follows the path of a wandering cowboy in the American West.

Once again I have my Cowboy Artist pard Al P. Bringas along for the ride, bringing graphic illustrations to this bygone era.

Kick up a chair or sit back easy in that saddle seat, thumb a chapter or two, and enjoy *T. H. Elkman: A Western Novel.*

Sincerely,

Eric H. Heisner

Chapter 1

In the southern region of New Mexico territory, just to the east of Silver City, a heavily laden wagon rolls across terrain nearly mistakable for West Texas drylands. The bulky contents of the four-wheeled cart are concealed by an oiled tarp, tied down and tucked in at the edges. Aged, wood-spoked wheels pulled by a pair of long-legged mules slowly creak and grind their way over broken rock earth and low scrub brush. The team steadily leans into the harness as their ears twitch to the distant surroundings.

Atop the wagon bench sit two grown men and a half-breed Indian woman. Rough, brutal-looking characters, the menfolk each have a quid of tobacco packed in their grizzled cheek. Their stained whiskers are bung-full of the brown juices that drip from dry, cracked lips. Wearing heavy coats despite the warm temperature, the long barrel of a shotgun pokes from under the sprung wooden seat.

The woman sitting between them has a greasy black mane that hangs down in matted, Indian-style braids. She sways along, crowded between the oversized pair on the wagon bench. The heat of the mid-day sun thickens the air around the group with a strong heavy odor and she shows no emotion or objection to their foul scent in her unattached, deep-set, and dark staring eyes.

The wagon creaks and rattles along under the steady pull of the mule team and one of the men pivots to look over his shoulder. His one good eye, set next to a milky glazed-over pupil, scans the surrounding hills. He puckers his cheek and shoots a stream of brown spittle arching over the turning wheel into the brush beyond. Scratching at bugs beneath his coat, he turns forward feeling satisfied with his survey of the territory.

A lone cowboy sits next to a smoldering fire and stares out to the morning sky. He turns his head slightly at the sound of movement behind him and eyes his dun-colored horse and pack animal as they nudge one another away from a tuft of dry grass.

Dressed in tall leather boots, a wide-brimmed hat, and scarf-bandana gently blowing at his neck, Tomas H. Elkman is a drifting cowboy of the times. He wears rough weave canvas britches that show wear from use with dark stains marking work under leather chaps. His vest and drop-sleeved shirt, having been worn together for too long, have each begun to take on the hue of the other.

Elkman smooths the full whiskers of his mustache and narrow chin beard with his fingertips, sweeping around his mouth. The long-sprouted beard stubble on his cheeks marks the passage of time away from urban civilization. He rubs a forefinger on his thumb then wipes it between his lips to cleanse grinning teeth of the nighttime taste. Elkman spits into the remaining coals of fire and stands to stretch his lean body in the morning light.

One man alone, Elkman gazes around in every direction. He takes in the vast open countryside and quiet solitude of his wandering lifestyle. The brightness of the morning sun and a gentle breeze of cool air sweeps over him. He watches a small bird flit from bush to scrub tree, then perch to scan about with jerky head twitches. Elkman takes a deep, holding breath, accepting of his lot in life. He lets go the lungful of air and tries to quell the ubiquitous longing for something more that seems to echo down somewhere inside. The quiet peacefulness of freedom is offset by the endurance to withstand loneliness.

A shadowy figure on a stout, big-footed black horse crests a ridge. The shaggy hooved beast stands firm as the man looks down on the tarp-covered wagon and the three occupants pressed together on the driver's bench. From above, he watches unmoved as the wagon crosses the terrain heading north. The team of mules step out at a steady, unhurried pace, occasionally ushered on by the slap of leather harness reins. Shaded by the broad brim of his hat, the dark-featured man leans down on the hefty plate horn of his Mexican saddle and peers into the distance.

Straightening a bit on his mount, he slides the floppy sugarloaf sombrero back on his pale forehead and lets long strands of hair gently blow past his face. He watches awhile longer, then looks at the midday sun over his shoulder and turns back. With hard-worn, knuckled fingers, he parts his overhanging lip whiskers to reveal a yellow, corn-toothed smile.

Elkman maneuvers his dun horse through the landscapes of rocky hills and deep ravines. He gives the pack animal's lead rope a tug as they move down a steep narrow grade. Gravel and larger rocks tumble and roll as the unshod hooves dig in for surer footing.

Coming up unscathed at the canyon floor, Elkman holds his animals and dallies the lead rope to the pack animal around his saddle horn. The leisurely paced cowboy tips his hat back and wipes the sweat from his temples with the cuff on his shirtsleeve. He looks around and feels unhurried from a lack of schedule or timelines. Elkman lifts his wooden canteen and gives it a slight jiggle before removing the cork stopper. He takes a short swallow of the warm contents and rehangs the water-streaked vessel over the saddle horn near his knee.

A slight breeze blows through the ravine as Elkman reaches into his vest pocket and pulls out tobacco fixings and rolling papers. He hooks one leg over the saddle and lets it dangle across his horse's neck. Quiet and patient, he takes his time assembling the rolled smoke.

The screech of a hawk overhead and Elkman glances up to the clear cloudless sky as he draws a match from his lower vest pocket. He strikes it with his thumbnail and tucks his head, lighting the hand-rolled paper perched between his lips. The smell of dry burning leaf and singed lip whiskers waifs down the canyon as the cowboy sits and listens to the emptiness in the breeze.

Elkman readjusts his hat, swings his leg back across the saddle, and takes the lead-rope in hand. He looks around the dry rocky canyon and nudges the dun horse forward, continuing on.

The wagon continues to creak along as one of the large burly men glances to the outline of an observant rider on the ridge. He grumbles unintelligibly under his breath and the Indian woman leans down and grabs up the long barreled shotgun from near her feet. The other man pushes his heavy coat aside to reveal a large framed percussion revolver holstered at his hip. A trickle of brown saliva trickles from the corner of his mouth as he sends another long arch of tobacco spittle to the ground. The driver shifts slightly in the seat and continues on with a slap of the reins.

Silhouetted, the man on the stout horse descends from the ridge and lopes the big footed animal toward the loaded supply cart. The men on the wagon watch the man's approach and the driver tugs leather lead lines back firmly causing the labored mule team to stop easy. As the man on horseback nears the wagon, the soft, muted sound of a rifle hammer being pulled back clicks heavily. The Indian woman glances at the man to her left and his hollow eyes shift while he holds a brass framed Henry rifle across his lap.

The three sit in the wagon seat and wait for the man's approach in the growing heat of the day. They stare as the mysterious character in the wide sombrero slides his mount to a halt before them. He walks his horse around to the near side of the wagon and tips his broad-brimmed hat back as if to say hello.

One of the men in the wagon nods with recognition toward the horseback visitor as he relaxes the aim of his rifle. Not a word is uttered as the figure in the wide sombrero angles his horse toward the sun. The light cuts a shadowed line below his eyes and catches his long, wispy lip-whiskers as they pull back to reveal that unique bandit smile.

Chapter 2

The evening sky is golden as it shimmers off the surrounding red sand and rocky bluffs. Elkman sits horseback, watching as dark carrion birds hover in the distance, circling and dropping from view. He studies the scene awhile and contemplates the likelihood of some sort of demise and decay. Elkman glances back at his pack animal while it tugs the lead rope closer to an edible shrub. As the animal raises its head, the cowboy mumbles to himself.

"Well, something got itself kilt over there."

The self-reliant cowboy instinctively puts his fingers to the dark walnut handle of the cartridge conversion pistol at his side. Eyes on the horizon, he lifts it from the snug leather holster an inch and lets it set high for an easy pull.

Elkman rides at a brisk walk through the scrubby, rock strewn terrain and covers the distance in short order. Crossing a single set of horse prints, he comes on two half-torn bodies being fought over and ripped at by coyotes clashing with the swooping buzzards overhead. He reins up, pulls his pistol and sends a shot into the air. The blood-faced scavengers look up at him hesitantly as he swings a leg over and slides from his mount.

"Go on . . . git!"

The horse shies from the hungry dogs and Elkman pulls down the leather reins to ground-tie the animal.

"Easy there, boy . . ."

Elkman steps closer and lets off another round from his pistol, scattering the feral dogs to the brush and sending the bald-headed fowl to flight.

The warmth of the afternoon mixed with the pungent smell of death puts a slight pallor to the onlooker's complexion. Elkman wipes the sweat from his cheek as he studies the slain bodies of two large men, both having been unceremoniously scalped. He covers his mouth with the back of his hand, winces in disgust, and quickly scans the immediate setting. The quiet barrenness of nature echoes between the bluffs and Elkman listens intently. With a quiet, steely gaze, he watches his surroundings for any sign of ambush or aggression.

Not far from the two bodies Elkman notices a pair of deep set wagon tracks. He kneels down to inspect the trail and discerns two harness animals and a single, big-footed horse coming along behind. He peers up to a shadow overhead as a carrion bird swoops down to brave a landing but hops a short distance off to another purpose.

The horse and pack animal stand patient as Elkman returns and steps around to the right-hand side of his mount. He holsters his pistol and slides his slab-sided Winchester rifle from the leather saddle scabbard. He levers in a cartridge and slowly moves toward the vulture's target.

A slight breeze blows away the stillness hanging on the landscape. Elkman stands and looks down over a third corpse. He studies the round-hipped form of a female body in filthy men's clothing, then a pair of dark Indian braids splayed out with a bullet hole between. He looks up to watch the birds slowly circle in the sky and stares into the empty horizon.

The town of Acworth, New Mexico, is a mix of canvas tents, wood buildings, and old stone missionary structures. Situated in the valley between the Mogollon and Elk Mountain ranges, the streets of the mid-sized burg are scattered with wagons, horses, and people. A haze of dust hangs in the air from the dry dirt road.

Easing his horse to a respite at the edge of town, Elkman sits and observes. His two animals eye the activity in town then cock a hind leg to wait for instruction. Elkman leans his forearm across the saddle horn and motions to a cowhand passing afoot.

"Eah, eah, fella. You been workin' these parts much?"

"Yaugh, been working fer the Deuce Fork for the winter."

Elkman nods and wipes his forefinger under his mustache. "Know if the lead man's been lookin' for an extra hand?"

"Naw, don't think so. Ya might check o'er at Amon's place jest north o' here. They was needin' extra help once."

The cowhand kicks a dried horse apple and it rolls across the gravely street. He looks up at Elkman and winces in the sunlight.

"If I hear anything, who should I say's lookin'?"

"Name's T. H. Elkman."

The cowhand nods and passes down the street leaving Elkman not the better for information. Nudging his spurred heels to hide, Elkman guides his horse down the busy street and stops before one of the larger drinking and entertainment establishments.

He looks up to the hand painted panel over the double doors and panes of glass windows. The sign has a drawing of a tall, bent over yellow-colored pine tree holding a single red apple from its branches. Elkman smiles curiously and murmurs to himself as he reads. "The Yaller Pine Apple Saloon . . ."

The horseback cowboy loops a dally tie around his saddle horn with the lead rope to his pack animal and swings a leg over to step down from his horse. He wraps his reins around a porch support post and looks toward the inviting saloon doors.

The activity in the street continues as Elkman strides up the wooden boardwalk, loosens his coat and gives it a dust-freeing shake. He stands before the wood-slatted swinging doors and adjusts the angle of his hat. With a hint of a keen smile escaping his lips, he steps inside.

Above the bar, which stretches the length of the room, hangs another fancier hand-painted sign featuring the image of The Yellow Pine Apple Saloon. Below the sign reads an advertisement for the quality of the establishment's recreational women, and a thin layer of smoke drifts through the mostly empty space from the few lit oil lamps. He looks around the saloon as the quiet murmur of voices at the back table breaks the near silence.

Elkman walks to the bar and pulls off his thick heavy coat. He drapes the covering over the bar-top and hooks his boot heel on the brass foot-rail. A bartender moves toward him and Elkman taps his fingers on the wooden slab before him with a solid thud.

"Sir, set me up with a mug."

The barkeep nods, grabs up a glass tankard and draws a brew from the staved barrel keg. He fills the vessel until the thick piling of foam overflows the lip of the glass and cranks off the wooden tap. He glances over his shoulder at Elkman while he cuts the lather along the top with a paddle knife.

"Lookin' fer anything else?"

"Jest something to quit the thirst."

The bartender turns and sets the mug of beer before Elkman.

"This stuff is made right here in town. Ya won't get any better or fresher than this."

The thick head on top of the dark amber liquid sits heavy, and the barkeep watches it proudly. "You be sure to let me know if you are needin' any type of services from the house."

Smiling, he lifts his chin toward the sign implying ladies for rent.

Elkman takes up the glass mug, sips off the top, and wipes his mustache with his fingertips.

"Much obliged."

The sound of giggling at the back wall catches Elkman's attention and he turns to the nearly vacant room. Two old men sit and drink quietly in one corner, staring at the other. Elkman's gaze travels to another table where a stout, well-dressed man regales two saloon girls with blustery boasting.

The bearded and oversized presence of Jefferson McGredy entertains the women as he kicks up his high-top black boots on the table's surface and pulls one of the ladies to his lap. She runs her fingers through the smiling man's long-groomed crop of chin whiskers and tries to tickle his nose with the ends like a brush.

Elkman watches the interactions of the broad gestured gentleman and gives a nod toward one of the ladies when she throws him a smile. Their gaze remains for a moment until it catches the watchful eye of McGredy. The brawny showman sizes up the cowboy at the bar for a quick second then waves him over.

"Hey, you, fella . . . come 'ere! You ever punched cattle?"

Elkman takes a sip of his beer and realizes his attentions to the engaged lady have been called out.

"Yaugh . . . I done my share."

McGredy scoots the gal off his lap and sits upright as his voice booms across the room.

"I was jest tellin' these fine ladies that a man could sneak up on one of them long-horned beasts, kiss 'em, and not get one of them brush stickers stuck in 'em, if'n he did it right."

Laying his heavy coat over his arm, Elkman holds his glass handled beer mug and moves closer to the table.

"And how might that be?"

Tilting his chair back, with a smile, McGredy acts the scene out through a whirl of motion.

"I figure that if ya sneak up on 'em, real careful like . . . grab 'em by the tail and yank it over its head good . . ."

McGredy suddenly reaches back and grabs one of the girls on the posterior with a fistful of skirting like a tail.

"Yank it hard till she's good and puckered up . . . then ya lay a big kiss on 'em!"

Pulling the saloon gal close, he lays a big bearded kiss on her. Surprised, but entertained, both of the painted up ladies burst into laughter and Elkman shakes his head, amused.

"Wouldn't want to be the poor sap that tried it 'less it was as nice lookin' as she is."

McGredy lets his rustled victim free, juts out his forefingers from the side of his head like a bull cow and bellows comically.

"I've kissed worse, I'll tell ya!"

Chapter 3

The late sun of afternoon has set in through the wavy, front glass panel windows. Many types of cowboy, townspeople, and gambler now fill the drinking hall of the Yellow Pine Apple Saloon. Elkman and McGredy play cards at the back table and seem to have the preponderance of female attentions compared to the rest of the occupants in the room. Several saloon patrons steal lusty glances at Elkman's table and the three working gals on McGredy's flank.

An old hardened cowboy deals the cards around the table and Elkman takes them up in his palm. He sorts through the dealt hand and keeps them close to his vest as one of the sporting gals shimmies over and pushes the brim of his hat up on the side. She whispers loudly in his ear.

"Hey, ya whiskered saddle bum. How 'bout we git upstairs fer a wash 'nd a tickle?"

With a shiver, Elkman holds his cards face-down on the table and leans his head away. He takes a gulp of beer from the near-empty mug and smiles sidelong at her.

"Thank ya kindly, ma'am. No thanks."

McGredy grunts, pleased as he studies his cards in hand.

"Hell bud, the way you been drinkin' and playing cards, ya might as well. I figure yer yearnin's already past yer earnin's . . . or ya got more money than spunk."

The cowhand dealer glances up at Elkman and gestures. "Yer bet."

Elkman takes up his cards again and shrugs. "Always figured it's bet'er to be dead drunk than dead hungry . . . or sober between the sheets of a rental."

McGredy laughs in a fit of amusement until a large, heavy-booted man walks up from behind and gives him a jolting nudge. The gambler's eyes dart over his shoulder at the clumsy lout and his bearded grin forms a scowl. "Excuse *you*, fella..."

"They call me Simon 'Eight-Foot' Burns and you's both gonna be *dead drunks* if ya don't stop crowdin' them womenfolk." The oversized aggressor gives an awkward smile down to the startled ladies at the table, trying to sway their attentions. A hard manner sweeps over McGredy's features as his stare burns into his hand of cards. Without looking behind at Simon Burns, he sets his jaw and murmurs low and firm.

"You best back off Mister . . . or I'll be knockin' a foot off the top 'nd puttin' my boot to yer hide."

Elkman looks up at the hulking mass of a man standing opposite, dwarfing the broad shoulders of McGredy. The unshaven beard and grime-stained clothing gives off the man's trade as some sort of teamster or hide-scraper. With fists the size of beef hocks and eyes deep set in a heavy brow, Elkman sizes up the colossal, rough-looking character. He clears his throat and tries his best to diffuse the tension.

"Now Mister, we're just having a friendly game here with some fine ladies. Why don't you go find yer seat again."

Simon looms over McGredy and clomps his heavy feet on the floor behind the gambler's chair while he paces and growls.

"Jest 'bout every one of 'em gals in the place are crowdin' here 'cept Squirrel-tooth Sal. Don't seem fair. Git up 'nd leave or give 'em over."

Elkman scoots his chair back a tad and glances around the fully crowded and bustling saloon. He recognizes the big man's argument and shrugs. "The ladies choose their own attentions and I don't recall anyone invitin' yer company."

Simon spits his words with a challenging tone. "I wasn't askin'!"

McGredy grunts and raises his beer mug to take a drink just as Simon passes behind and gives him another hostile shove. The thick glass mug swings past McGredy's lips and over the card table without spilling a drop. Elkman cocks his head, annoyed, and stares up at the large provoker who keeps angling for a fight.

"Now Mister . . ."

The chatter in the room begins to fade away as McGredy's chair scoots back with a rattle of wooden legs on plank floor. Elkman watches as McGredy stands and looks up at the tall-framed brute. The seemingly calm gambler takes a slow sip of beer from his nearly full mug, starts to turn away, then swings out and smashes the glass handled tankard into Simon's face.

The glass vessel explodes across the big man's jaw in a hail of glass shards and beer foam, sending the teamster to the floor in a heap. The room falls completely quiet and Elkman leans over, peering around the table at Simon "Eight-Foot" Burns lain out on the wood plank floor.

"I guess he was askin' fer it."

McGredy looks around with only the broken glass mug handle in his hand. He shrugs and half-smiles innocently. The room's stillness is broken suddenly when four similarly dressed teamsters break from the crowd and tackle McGredy. Knocked to the floor and pounded by whirling fists, the gambler struggles to break from the group and finally manages to regain his feet.

Fists flying, swinging out and fighting instinctively, McGredy smashes his knuckles into the nose of one of his aggressors, exploding it with a splash of blood. He catches an assailant's punch and swings him around to another attacker, knocking the two back into the crowd. Hooking his elbow back, McGredy clips one man under the chin and turns, slamming his knee in the exposed man's midsection. McGredy hammers his clenched fist on the back of the man's skull and the pummeled body drops to the floor in a heap.

The bar patrons slowly back away as McGredy stands in the room heaving and whirling like a hunted buffalo on defense. Blowing and panting for air, McGredy watches the crowd for his next attacker. The gambler gives a slight satisfied glance toward Elkman when he notices the large man, Simon Burns, slowly rising from the floor near their vacant table. McGredy takes two skipping steps and delivers a swift-booted punt to the bloodied man's face then turns back to the bout.

The battered aggressors close in on him again and blows are traded evenly. McGredy stands four feet of ground as the brawlers take alternating goes at him. Gradually, the fighting men start to tire of the fruitless contest while the teamster with the broken nose drops away and falls into a nearby chair.

McGredy, looking disheveled but not too much worse for wear, gains a second wind and roars victorious at his attackers.

"Come on ya chicken-shit bastards! Step up and git some more. Only fight I'll have is getting' yer stink off my fists."

The boastful gambler does an Irish jig dance and whirls his fists around in a display of fist-to-cuffs. The amused crowd laughs and pushes the reluctant teamsters back into the fray. McGredy fakes with his right and pops one of the men with his left to the raucous cheers of the onlookers.

Away from the circling crowd, without being noticed, Simon Burns climbs from the floor and quickly grabs up a round wooden game table.

Before anyone registers the sight of a tabletop and four wooden legs hovering airborne, McGredy turns to have the furniture come crashing down on him.

Knocked off balance and reeling back into a set of chairs, McGredy tumbles and hits the floor. Simon and the others are quickly upon him with the pounding of fists. McGredy covers his face and kicks out with his legs trying to get some separation from the flailing blows.

Observing the troublesome gambler at a severe disadvantage, Elkman steps forward from the crowd. He grabs hold of one of the teamsters from the scuffle, after the man delivers a cheap kick, and jabs him in the gut. The brawler doubles over gasping for breath and Elkman rams his head into the wooden bar-side with a thud. He shoves him back against Simon Burns and the two fighters topple over. McGredy is able to momentarily regain his feet and sends a hard right jab into the side of Simon's head as he rises.

McGredy stands in a daze and swings wildly. The crowd pulls back as the fight becomes a melee of stumbling blows. Simon Burns is punched back into the onlookers and wipes his large hand across his bloodied mouth. He spits a steam of crimson spittle with fractions of broken teeth and eyes a loose pistol kicked across the floor.

Simon reaches down, grabbing up the firearm and rips off a shot that deafens the room. McGredy looks at the bullet splintered wood next to him on the bar-top and all is quiet a moment as he turns to the gun-toting hulk. His jaw slacks and eyes fill with cautionary panic as Simon wipes his face again and charges at him with the pistol raised.

McGredy quickly backs up and dives over the bar, rolling behind as Simon fires another shot. The crowd scurries away as Simon stands before the bar waving the gun and hollering.

"Com'n out here, ya damned coward! Look at what ya did to my face . . . I'm gonna kill you!"

Simon smears blood from the cuts on his lips and cheek and tosses it off like tears. He fires again and shattered bottles and spilt whiskey crumble down the bar-back. Elkman puts his hand to the butt of his revolver while Simon advances on the wooden barrier, hammering lead slugs into it.

Suddenly McGredy leaps up from behind the bar with the Barkeep's scattergun held just above waist level. Simon raises the pistol at the offending gambler, cocking it again and letting the hammer fall with an empty click. His face fills with momentary horror and dread as McGredy lets go with both barrels of buckshot. The large man's body stumbles back a few steps, crushing a table as it falls to the floor.

McGredy stands behind the bar and glances down at the twin smoking barrels of the shotgun.

"Now look at the rest of ya . . ."

Tossing the shotgun aside, McGredy climbs over the bar-top and looks down at Simon "Eight-Foot" Burns. The hulking teamster is nearly cut in half, lying bloody and splayed over the broken table.

"You damn dirty coward . . ."

The room hangs in quiet shock as McGredy rushes over to collect his belongings. Two of the dead teamster's associates jerk their pistols and Elkman quickly draws and fires twice. The explosions from his handgun hit one of the men in the shoulder, the other in the forearm and they both drop their guns to the floor in thudding unison.

McGredy ducks down behind the table and peeks up at the two injured men. He huffs as he peers over at Elkman.

"Cripes . . ."

Elkman watches as McGredy grabs the money from the pot in the center of the table and scurries toward the rear entrance.

"Where the hell you goin'?"

McGredy glances over his shoulder, pauses a moment, then continues on out the back.

"Me and the law don't have an understandin' of each other. You stay and tell 'em what happened."

Elkman quickly slips his pistol back in the holster, grabs up his coat and moves toward the double front entry doors.

"The hell with that . . ."

The two hastily exit opposite ends of the drinking establishment, leaving the confusion of the crowd and a haze of black powder smoke behind.

Chapter 4

Outside the Yellow Pine Apple Saloon, Elkman quickly inspects his saddled horse and pack animal. He unties his mount and tosses the reins over the horse's neck. About to step into the stirrup, Elkman turns to see McGredy coming from the alley around the side corner of the building. The fleeing gambler emerges with his saddle gear and horse in tow.

McGredy pulls his fidgety mount over next to Elkman and smiles. "Figured you'd have 'nough sense not to stick 'round."

Elkman steps into the stirrup and swings his other leg over the saddle. He takes up the reins and looks down at McGredy.

"Enough sense not to stick 'round you."

News of the commotion begins to spread through town and Elkman backs his horse away from the front of the saloon. He observes at the far end of the main dirt street, two city-dressed men with official looking badges and sawed-off scatterguns leading a small grouping of spectators.

He watches them a moment as they move along the boardwalk toward the saloon at a brisk business-like pace.

"If yer not wantin' to speak with the law 'nd explain yerself, ya best hurry it along."

McGredy dances around his horse trying to get the blanket straight and his saddle over the back of the skittish animal.

"Aww, dammit! Come on you bastard . . . shit, hold still!"

Glancing back at the approaching lawmen, Elkman gives his horse a prod and trots away in the opposite direction.

The street becomes a buzz of excitement as several occupants of the saloon carry the news through town. Elkman peers over his shoulder past his trailing pack animal at McGredy who finally gets his horse under control and saddled.

The gambler keeps his head low behind his mount as the two town law-officers pass by him and step inside the Yellow Pine Apple Saloon. Throwing his coat over the saddle pommel, McGredy climbs into the seat and adjusts his hat. The disheveled gambler sits his horse, glances toward the entry of the saloon, and pats his vest pocket holding his collected table winnings.

The front batwing doors of the saloon swing open and the lawmen reemerge, scanning the street and walkway. They exchange a discerning glance with McGredy and motion for him to dismount. With a dismissive gesture, McGredy instantly hunkers down and gives his horse the spurs. An echoing blast of a shotgun turns Elkman to glance back one last time to see McGredy galloping through town.

As Elkman passes the last building at the edge of town civilization, he gives his pack animal's lead rope a tug and urges his animals to a loping canter. The sound of gunshots and yelling behind him, he curses under his breath mumbling to himself.

"Gol-dammed ass head has me runnin' out of town . . ."

The afternoon light has burned on toward evening and Elkman walks ahead, leading his two sweated animals. In the distance he sees a trail of red dust rising, headed in his direction. Elkman pulls his rifle from the saddle scabbard and watches the rider's steady approach. Eyes squinted,

Elkman studies the horseback form awhile and recognizes the figure of the troublesome gambler. He shakes his head with disgust, keeps his rifle in hand, and leads his animals along, continuing afoot.

Coming along at a hard gallop, McGredy thunders up and pulls his lather-caked horse to a sliding stop next to Elkman. Gravel and sand kick up from under metal-shod hooves and streaks of perspiration drip from the horse's flank. McGredy beams like a child who got away with stealing a pie.

"Hey there, pard. That was one hell ov'a ride!"

Elkman stops and observes that both McGredy and his mount are beat and near worn out from hard riding.

"You best cool that mount and saddle that horse proper if ya want him to last."

McGredy heaves a breath of air and grins as he steps down next to Elkman. He unties the loose cinch and pulls the ill-fitted saddle and blanket to the ground. Ekman watches the horse's muscles tremble and the soon-to-be sore spots lathered in foam. He glances to McGredy who pulls his coat from the saddle heap and dusts it off, more concerned with his wardrobe than the horse's well-being. He shakes his head, annoyed, and continues leading his two animals.

McGredy looks to the evening sky and eases into his coat. He notices Elkman moving away and calls out.

"Hold up for a bit."

Elkman keeps walking and doesn't look back as he calls out, "I've had quite 'nuf of yer company. Ya likely have a posse after you."

"I circled 'round 'nd watched for 'em. The path I took was so irregular I don't think I could follow it back again."

"Too bad."

McGredy leads his horse and pulls his gear along the ground.

"Hell, from what I saw, it was looking as if you were havin' a good time back there."

Elkman stops and deliberately turns to look back at McGredy.

"Didn't mind till I had to draw 'nd shoot them two. Being pushed into that sort of thing don't sit well with me."

The smile falls from McGredy's face and he shrugs, unconcerned.

"Ya should of jest kilt them. They was gonna murder me in cold blood given the chance."

Elkman reaches over his horse's neck and sheaths his rifle in the leather scabbard. He flips up a stirrup, hooks it on the saddle horn, and checks his cinch for snugness.

"Takin' a man's life don't make no softer pill'er at night."

"They got off bett'r than they deserved."

Elkman drops and smooths the leather skirting down, then steps into the stirrup and sits the saddle.

"Most of us do . . . and a lot better than that other fella."

McGredy looks slightly ashamed and kicks a rock with his boot.

"Yaugh, guess so."

Looking downcast, McGredy watches as Elkman starts to ride down the trail. He looks down at his saddle on the ground and hollers after the departing cowboy.

"Hey, ya mind if I ride along with ya 'nd share a fire tonight? There's Indians and such in these parts."

Elkman halts his horse, pauses to think about the consequences of McGredy's companionship, and finally turns in the saddle.

"I ain't the law, so's I guess yer free to do as ya please. Figured I'd camp up yonder if you've got a mind to come along."

Continuing on, Elkman rides toward a distant cluster of tree-lined boulders backed by rocky bluffs. McGredy grabs up his gear, swings the blanket over his mount, and saddles up proper.

A small fire crackles and pops, stabbing up into the chilled moonlit night. Elkman lies back against his saddle gear and leans on an elbow looking across the flames toward McGredy. He glances past the gambler to the horses hobbled nearby just at the edge of the firelight. McGredy maneuvers a silver coin through his fingers and smiles when he catches Elkman taking notice.

"You ain't spoke a word to me for quite a spell. You ain't still sore 'bout what happened in town are ye?"

Elkman looks skyward and inhales the cool night air. A shimmer catches his eye and he watches as McGredy flips the coin in the firelight and stealthily slips it back into his vest pocket. The bearded gambler smiles and displays his disarming charm.

"Name is Jefferson McGredy. Titled after Tom Jefferson but my Ma said it might as well have been after Ol' Davis."

Elkman pulls out his fixings, carefully rolls a smoke, and lights it. He sits quietly awhile, exhales a small puff, and looks at McGredy.

"Tomas H. Elkman."

"What's the 'H' stand for?"

"Jest holds up between names."

McGredy makes an understanding roll of his eyes and looks to the smoke of the small campfire.

"We all got our secrecies."

"Some more'n others."

The two sit in silence for several minutes until McGredy can't stand the quiet anymore.

"Which way ya headed?"

"Whichever the way, I'd like to make it where I'm going alive and clear of the law."

"I guess I could do my best to keep you out of trouble."

Elkman takes a final drag on the hand-rolled smoke and shakes his head, doubtful.

"I feel you tend to git into trouble just about anywheres."

"A little trouble never killed anyone."

Glancing up, Elkman gives the gambler a knowing look. McGredy shrugs and pokes the fire a bit.

"I guess some do get kilt, but it hasn't got me yet."

Elkman tosses away his smoke and leans back on his saddle.

"I don't want to be anywhere near when trouble enough comes along to kill you."

McGredy shakes his head with a smile. "Hell, I don't either."

The camp is quiet with exception to the sounds of night. Elkman relaxes easy as the glow from the warming flames lights up the two men's features on either side of the campfire. He thinks awhile and notices as McGredy steals occasional glances toward him. Adjusting his hat, Elkman gives a cough and finally speaks.

"I'll let you trail with me if yer needin' till I find some work at one of them ranches north o' here. After that, yer on your own cause I don't want to be takin' care of no one but myself."

McGredy seems slightly offended at the offer.

"No need to be disagreeable 'bout it. I just figure it's safer traveling by two in these parts. You know with the Indians, bandits, renegades and such."

"I've had no trouble."

McGredy tosses another stick on the fire and puffs up.

"Bet ye like to keep it that way too!"

"Sittin' in a saloon regular most likely, what would you know 'bout Injuns?"

"I've done some scouting 'nd Indian relations for the US government after the war. I'm acquainted with most areas north of here clear to Montanee. You'd do yerself wise to stick with my know'd and experienced ways."

Elkman nods and settles back deeper, ready for sleep. He wipes his upper lip whiskers away from his mouth and closes his eyes with a sigh. "Jest awhile then or till I find work."

Chapter 5

In the Colorado territory, south of the Mesa Verde, a new day crests on the vast open land. The coldness of morning hangs in the air and seeps through chilled clothing slowly warmed by the sun. Flexing his stiff fingers, Elkman pulls out the fixings for his habit and rolls up a smoke. He watches from atop his bedroll as McGredy handles a tin cup near the small fire stoked from the coals of the evening's cooked meal.

McGredy swirls the dark contents of the cup hoping for steam and takes a sip. "Aw, I can hardly stand cold coffee."

"Hot or cold, it does the same trick."

"Well, I'd ruther chew it warm."

Elkman shrugs and lights his hand-rolled. McGredy nestles his metal cup with the coffee in the warm embers near the low flame and sets another stick on the fire. He briskly rubs his hands together for warmth and scratches his whiskered cheek.

"I've been thinking 'bout you headin' north. Now that the winter's 'bout o'er up there, I know a gal in Montana territory who I've been meanin' to git back to."

Elkman leans back on an elbow and looks at McGredy.

"N'er said I was going *that* far north."

"Figured you might want to consider it. Beautiful country last time I was there and they was startin' all types of ranches. All of 'em needin' help too cause the lack of population 'nd abundance of land."

With the rolled tobacco hanging between his lips, Elkman takes an easy drag on the smoke and exhales. He kicks his booted feet out in front of him and crosses his arms to keep off the cold.

"McGredy, I've only known you a short while, but I find it a bit odd that you'd go way up there fer a woman."

McGredy takes his cup from the bed of smoldering cinders, gives it a probing blow then sips.

"She's not jest any woman ya see. She ain't particular beautiful . . . but, well . . . she's special."

"How's that? Cain't be that good a cook."

Hiding his mouth behind the steaming cup, McGredy glances over the metal rim at Elkman.

"Naugh, nothin' like that. She's what you'd call wealthy."

Elkman sits up laughing and tosses away his smoke.

"And they say ye cain't buy love?"

"No, but it'll take ya a long ways with affection."

"Hell, I thought you were wantin' to go up there to get yerself hitched. I'd have no part in that."

Sitting back on his haunches just shy of his spurs, McGredy smiles and swirls the coffee in his cup.

"No, I couldn't do that and disappoint all the other women."

Elkman throws an amused glance toward the gambling man, rubs his hands over his vest and tucks them under his arms for warmth. McGredy rocks on his heels and grins.

"Besides, why buy the whole cow when ya git the freshest milk fer free?"

Elkman climbs to his feet, stares out at the beautiful vista of open landscape and adjusts his hat on his forehead.

"I've come to find that some men's wives are angels . . . 'nd t'others are still alive."

Thinking a moment, McGredy watches Elkman grab up his pack gear and head for the horses. He smiles and chuckles to himself, then tosses the dredges from his cup on the dying flames.

Traveling north, Elkman and McGredy ride along beside one another. The days amount to a week and landscapes change from high country scrub to trees and foothills coming toward mountains. The two men traveling horseback cross clear stream waters that flow down from the high country and spread out in wide, shallow washes.

Halfway across one of the water crossings, Elkman eyes an oddity hung up on the opposite bank. He steers his animals toward the snagged object and makes out the waterlogged form of a man's body, pale and limp. Prodding his horse to the edge of the river, Elkman rides cautiously to the figure and dismounts. Afoot, he looks around for any other signs of persons or possessions and stares down at the seemingly drowned man.

He turns as McGredy clops his horse toward the shallow water and stops a short distance away. McGredy peers at the body through the legs of Elkman's animals. "What'cha got there, pard?"

With cold mountain waters streaming around the ankles of his tall leather boots, Elkman bends down and rolls the mysterious body over. He puts his hand to the man's pale watery chest and seems surprised to find faint breath. Placing his fingers alongside the man's neck, Elkman feels for a pulse.

"He's still alive . . . ain't much, but still there."

Elkman gives his animals free rein and nudges them clear of the body to drink upstream. He calls up to McGredy, still horseback, who considers the situation warily.

"We pull 'em from this cold water and he may live. Ya suppose there's a settlement here abouts?"

McGredy eases his horse nearer and leans down on the saddle to get a closer examination. He eyes the man suspiciously and looks up at the wild natural landscapes all around.

"Don't know 'xactly where here is but I haven't seen a sign of folks nigh fer several days."

The emaciated man's wrinkled skin is almost translucent from the chill of the water. McGredy looks the man's body over and shakes his head skeptical.

"He can't be still alive? He looks all used up."

"Well, we ain't gonna bury him in the drink. Grab my animals, will ya."

Elkman pulls the limp, thin-framed body to edge of the river. He studies him and notices traces of sun blisters on his face and chest along with raw-worn rope burns on his wrists. He glances up at McGredy as he leads his animals ashore.

"Looks as if he's survived a lot worse than waterloggin'. Help me with him."

McGredy makes a distasteful face and shakes his head negative.

"Naw, I don't really like messing with that sort of thing."

Elkman looks up at McGredy and gives him a scolding glare. Unenthused, McGredy steps down from his horse and unties his blanket roll from behind the cantle. He shakes it out and helps Elkman lift the frail body onto it. With the wet body slung in the blanket, they carry the man up the bank toward higher ground and the shelter of trees.

McGredy grunts as his slick-soled boots slip on the wet rocky shore. "For being a skinny little runt, he sure do have heft. Must have soaked up half the river."

Elkman pulls the body up the riverbank, leading toward a decent spot to camp with trees overhead.

"Put 'em down here. Good place for a pause and easy digging if we need."

Dropping the foot end, McGredy stares down at his occupied blanket slightly perturbed.

"I don't much like having a dead man in my sleepin' blanket. We could have buried him down there."

Elkman squints at McGredy and pulls the blanket up around the limp man as the frail form begins to shiver.

"Go 'nd git the horses. I'll make up a fire"

Spitting to the ground, McGredy grumbles as he walks away to gather the animals.

The afternoon sun begins to drop to the mountains and cast long shadows through the trees. McGredy sits near the campfire, uneasy, as Elkman tends to the body. He leans back from the smoke as his trail partner tucks the blanket tight around the barely breathing man then stands and goes to the horses.

Watching Elkman unsaddle his mount, McGredy glowers at his blanket on the almost dead man. The irritated gambler scratches his beard and grunts.

"I guess he ain't dead yet?"

"Not yet."

"I wonder where that feller came from."

Elkman pulls his saddle down and carries it along with his blanket and rifle over near the fire. He lays out the blanket and saddle then leans the rifle over the propped up cantle.

"He's lucky he didn't drown."

"He's damned lucky to be still in my blanket."

"You can take it back if it spites you so."

Keenly aware of McGredy's sour mood, Elkman returns to his horse and unburdens his pack animal.

McGredy eyes his blanket wrapped around the man again and spits into the fire. He waves the drifting smoke away and hollers toward Elkman as he works nearby.

"Indians must have got hold of 'em, I figure."

Elkman stands and looks over at the swaddled form.

"Could be."

The perceptive gambler eyes one of the man's thin hands protruding from the blanket.

"I've seen wrists rubbed raw like that, 'cept they was on a corpse still staked to the ground."

"Should know soon enough if he's gonna make it or not."

McGredy shakes his head again with growing frustration.

"I ain't gonna sit around these parts playing wet nurse to a near-dead man."

Elkman finishes piling his gear and tending the horses then walks over and squats near the small campfire.

"We'll camp here for the night. If he's still with us in the morning, we'll pack 'em along to the nearest town."

"You mean to bring him with us?"

"Only if he's still drawin' breath."

"Gol-damn, that's the silliest thing I ever heard."

"What would you have us do?"

McGredy looks over at the wisp of a man as his chest trembles with scant breath. "Leave 'em."

"For dead?"

"Hell, we're puttin' him a lot better off than he was floatin' face down in the river."

Elkman places a few more sticks on the fire and scoots back to lean on his saddle seat.

"We ain't tied, McGredy. You're welcome to go yer own way at any time. I won't leave a man to die without good reason."

McGredy chews his lip whiskers and glares over at the body and his only warm blanket.

"There is something about him I sure don't like."

Elkman sits back and opens his war bag.

"You're a good judge of character I guess?"

"It's part of my trade. I kin sniff trouble when it's on me."

Drawing a wrapped bundle from the sack, Elkman takes out some hard-tack bread. He tosses a crumbling piece to McGredy and chews off a mouthful.

"We'll come to find out in the mornin' I guess."

McGredy hunches his shoulders and bites into the hard biscuit.

"Yeah, we'll know one way t'other I reckon."

Chapter 6

Elkman and McGredy continue riding north, trailing the human cargo in poor health. The new passenger sits slumped and secured behind the supplies on the pack animal. He flops around, mostly hunched over the canvas covered pack saddle but tied firmly around his bottom half. McGredy slows his horse and watches the limp man as he sits unconscious astride the burdened animal.

"Sure don't look comfortable flopping around like that."

Elkman glances back at the man, then McGredy.

"Was the best I could do without hog-tie'n him."

"Hell, what was to happen if yer animal gets mischievous 'nd wants to roll or get tangled up?"

Elkman shrugs.

"He'll still be there, he's tied well."

McGredy grunts, half-smiling as he trots his horse past the pack animal and up alongside Elkman.

"Yeah, at least his bottom half would be."

The terrain rises before them in wooded bluffs and rock-stacked ledges. The two horsemen and the unconscious figure ride along silently until something suddenly makes an awful throaty-choking sound, mixed between a dry-heave and a cough. McGredy looks to Elkman and gets a horrified look on his face as the sound lingers against the rock walls.

"What the hell was that?"

The gambler stops his horse and looks around questioningly.

"Did you hear that?"

Elkman pauses and holds back his mount. He glances to the surrounding cliffs and their emptiness echoes in the breeze.

"N'er heard anything like it."

They both look around and listen intently until they hear another dry heave crackle. McGredy looks to Elkman and motions with a disgusted gesture toward the man on the pack saddle.

"Hell . . . it's him."

Elkman nods and eases his horse back to study the near dead body hunched over his stowed gear.

"God, that's a terrible sound. What the hell do ya think is wrong with 'em?"

Scratching his chin whiskers, McGredy shrugs.

"Maybe he's got a hair biscuit."

"Give 'em some water."

McGredy lifts his canteen from his saddle horn, reaches over, and turns the limp man's head. He slowly pours some water from the canteen across the parched lips. The man slowly tongues his dry, chapped mouth, licking his moistened whiskers, and McGredy pours a bit more.

The man's body moves slightly then convulses in another dry heave hiss and McGredy leans away. He watches the man awhile as he coughs and sputters to life. McGredy shifts in the saddle and turns to exchange a curious look with Elkman.

"Jeez, that can't be good."

"Better'n being dead."

Coughing, the man weakly lifts his hand and reaches out for the water canteen. McGredy looks questioningly to Elkman who gives a consenting shrug.

"Give 'em some more."

McGredy hands the water container to the man as he attempts to prop himself upright, still coughing. The pair watches as the gaunt, near corpselike figure tips back the wooden jug and drinks hastily with most of the water running down his front. The vessel near empty, McGredy grunts and shakes his head as he takes back his canteen and jiggles the meager splash of liquid inside.

"For a fella nearly drowned, he sure has a thirst."

Elkman turns his horse and faces the emaciated man. He dallies off the lead rope for the pack animal and tries to make out the dark eyes through the tangled mop of hair.

"What's yer name fella?"

The hollow-eyed man tries to speak but the sounds only come out faint as a raspy garble. The effort seems to spend most of his energy and the man leans himself on the strapped pile of canvas-covered gear. Elkman cocks his head, uncertain, as the man seems to stare through him.

"How's that?"

McGredy snorts.

"I think he said *Graaal.*"

"Kinder sounded something like that."

The man coughs a bit more then lies his head down atop the pack saddle. He groans and turns his head away from the two men with a faint yellow, corn-toothed smile.

Elkman gathers wood for a fire as the sun looms behind thick gray clouds above. He looks to the campsite with the man rolled in McGredy's blanket and his ears perk at the sound of a gunshot in the distance. Elkman nods to himself in hopes that McGredy has secured them some fresh meat for dinner. Stepping into camp, Elkman drops an armful of firewood and looks to the strange survivor now in their company.

The stranger rolls over in the blanket and slowly sits up. He has a queer suspicious look to him that emanates from his squinty eyes and crooked mouth covered over in facial whiskers. A mess of long, greasy hair falls limply around pale, sunken features. He looks up at Elkman and heaves a shallow grunt.

"I take it I ain't dead?"

"Doesn't appear that way."

The man touches his sun-blistered cheek and notices the rope-worn raw spots just before his palm. He lowers his hand and covers his wrist self-consciously.

"Guess I was in pretty bad shape."

"Weren't sure you'd make it till now."

The man gazes away, avoiding eye contact and mumbles low.

"Thanks fer squarin' me up."

"You got a name?"

"Ye can call me Bob."

"Alright Bob, best to keep still for now and try to git some rest. McGredy will be back with some eats 'fore long."

Elkman squats near the wood pile and breaks small sticks to make a fire. Bob watches him awhile before lying back and curling up in the blanket. He scratches his boney fingers through his scraggly beard and coughs a chest-clearing fit before resting quiet. Elkman watches a moment and listens as the man's raspy breathing fades to an even pace.

Elkman draws a matchstick from his upper vest pocket and strikes it with his thumbnail. He stares across at Bob a moment until the flare settles, then he lights the small kindling and carefully tends the flame. Waving the smoke away, Elkman peers across the fire at the stranger and studies the man in apparent slumber.

A cool draft blows down from the high mountains and the clouded sun fails to ease the coming chill through the camp. The sound of the surrounding wood is strangely quiet as Elkman intuitively puts his hand to the butt of his revolver and gently leans down to blow into the growing flames.

Chapter 7

A fire crackles in the cool evening air. Elkman and McGredy eat at pieces of a pheasant-size bird roasted on a stick near the warming fire. The sky darkens as clouds pass over the rising moon. Picking at his teeth, McGredy grunts.

"What did he say again?"

"Not much of anything."

"He ain't moved 't all since I've been back. Sure he ain't dead? Sometimes they get a last spurt of vigor before they croak."

McGredy watches as Elkman removes a wing section of meat from the cooked bird with his knife.

"Could be."

"You ain't curious?"

Picking around the bones, Elkman chews slowly.

"Nope."

The firelight flares momentarily and McGredy looks over his piece of carcass for any edible remains. He picks at it then tosses it away into the darkness.

"Why?"

"Why what?"

McGredy wipes his hands on the underside of his saddle.

"Why ain't you curious?"

Elkman gives up chewing on the small wing and throws it away.

"When I talked with him brief, he didn't have anything interestin' to say."

"Didn't say how he got plopped in the river?"

Sliding fingers into his vest pocket, Elkman pulls out his makings for a smoke and hangs the string of the tobacco pouch from his teeth. "Guess he didn't figure it any of my business."

"Well, damn! Only reason I let you use my blanket for 'em was that maybe a good story would come of it."

Elkman glances up from under his hat brim then goes back to spreading and rolling his tobacco. "Probably still get somethin' out of 'em."

"I better. He's jest a damned waste of time so far." McGredy crosses his arms and sits back, pouting. "Should jest take my blanket and leave 'em back to nature is what I should do."

Elkman shrugs and lights up his smoke. Just outside the edge of the firelight, the frail body in McGredy's blanket stirs. Elkman lets an impish smile escape from behind his mustache.

"I hear a story brewing."

McGredy places more branches on the fire, building it up. The fire grows and the light reaches the curled up body of the mysterious man in the blanket. He stirs then coughs and rolls up on his elbow toward the two. "Don't have to build it up on my account."

"Sure, cause ye have my blanket," McGredy murmurs under his breath. He tosses a few more sticks on the fire and peers over at the shadowy, unkempt man looking back. The man sits up and the flames mirror off his dark glassy eyes.

"You the other feller who pulled me from the drink?"

"Yep. The owner of that there blanket yer wearin' too."

The man squints into the light and studies McGredy a moment. Staring at the burly gambler, side lit by the fire, no hint of recognition shows in the ragged man's face.

"Much obliged. The name's Robert Snarel." He glances over at Elkman as he sits smoking and observing. "Most just call me Bob."

Elkman smooths back his facial whiskers and spits a tiny piece of loose tobacco from his lip.

"How you feelin'?"

"Wouldn't happen to have anything to eat would you?"

Reaching over, Elkman picks up the stick with the rest of the cooked bird on it from next to the fire. He holds it out to Bob.

"Ain't much, but it quiets the rumblin'."

Shrugging the blanket from his shoulders, Bob scoots closer to the fire and eagerly takes it from Elkman's hand. Without much pause, he hungrily picks at the scant lingering of meat on the bones. McGredy watches as the skinny man chews and bites at the scrappy bird carcass like someone who hasn't eaten in some time. The watchful gambler tosses another stick on the fire and observes, interested.

"Where you from 'xactly?"

Bob gnaws at the small bones and looks up at McGredy, then over to Elkman. He sucks every speck of edible fragment from the small skeleton and wipes his whiskers.

"Louisiana."

McGredy grimaces at the curt answer and watches him continue ravaging the bird. Waiting for the man to suck the last bone clean, he continues his questioning.

"What brought you out here?"

Bob tosses the remaining scraps away, scoots back, and draws the blanket up around his shoulders. He looks over at McGredy who stares at him with a probing eye.

"I came west for business."

"What kind was that exactly?"

"Trade. Wares 'nd such."

McGredy nods, skeptical, and gazes toward Bob's raw rubbed wrists holding the blanket. Bob stares back at McGredy and tucks his hands out of view as he pulls the woolen wrap around him. They quietly glare at each other, neither speaking his mind. Elkman watches them both silently spar and lies back on his bedroll and saddle. "I'm gonna get some sleep."

Bob Snarel's features hint at a sly sneer as he pulls the warm covering tighter and looks to the fire. McGredy and Bob sit, silently staring at the flames as they burn down and glow red. McGredy's temper festers and he looks to the man wrapped snugly in his sole blanket. Bob glances at him and McGredy meets his gaze with a burning displeasure. With dark steely eyes shadowed by hollowed features, Bob speaks low.

"This yer blanket?"

"Yep."

"You mind me making use of it?"

McGredy puts another stick to the fire and pokes it sending sparks of embers skyward. Elkman peers out from under his lowered hat as McGredy speaks, slow and deliberate, keeping his mounting irritation under control.

"We gone and saved you from the brink of death. Can't let ya freeze in the night now can we?"

Bob Snarel picks at his teeth, staring into the flames then nods with a shifty glance toward McGredy. He adjusts the blanket around his shoulders and scoots a comfortable distance away from the fire before lying down. McGredy pokes the glowing coals again with perturbed contempt while glaring at the curled up body nestled in his blanket.

The stirred up firelight puts a golden glow on the surrounding woods and Elkman eases his hat down over his eyes. He settles in to sleep as McGredy grumbles under his breath, voicing his troubles into the quiet of night.

Chapter 8

The morning light creeps over the mountains and glints brilliantly on the surrounding treetops and rocks. Shivering near the dying ashen-embers from the night's fire, McGredy sits up and glares at Snarel. He blows his warming breath into stiff hands and tucks them close to his vest, under his elbows. He gives another agitated shiver and stirs the fire alive with a stick from the wood pile while he mumbles to himself quietly. "Sure could of used my damned blanket last night . . ."

McGredy watches as Elkman rolls from under his covering, scratches his mussed hair and sets his hat on. Elkman pulls on his tall boots, rises, and goes to his pack gear. He scoops ground coffee into a small tin pot and adds water from his canteen. Walking over to McGredy at the re-vived campfire, Elkman squats down on his haunches.

"Good mornin', McGredy."

"Cold is what it is." McGredy grunts and holds his hands tight under his arms.

The smoke from the moist tinder waifs past and Elkman nestles the pot next to the old coals and new flames. He sits close and warms his hands through the circling wisps of wood smoke. McGredy stares at the warming coffee mixture awhile then takes up his metal cup from his saddlebag nearby and rubs out the insides with his fingers.

"Damned near froze last night."

"Winter air still coming down from the mountains."

McGredy steals another agitated look toward Bob Snarel who slowly stirs awake. He shakes his head and grumbles.

"I ain't goin' another night freezin' my tail off."

Elkman nods and swirls the warming coffee in the pot. He glances over his shoulder as Bob sits up and scratches his mangy beard. "Mornin' Bob."

The peculiar man looks at his surroundings and seems relieved at the calm unmolested camp. He clears his weak throat and croaks out a greeting.

"Mornin' to yous both."

Protecting himself from the chill of daybreak, Bob holds the blanket tight around his shoulders, which irritates McGredy further. He scoots closer to the campfire and peers down at Elkman's tin cup.

"You have any 'xtry coffee for the likes of me?"

Elkman takes up his cup and pours some of the warmed coffee mixture, careful not to pour the grounds. He looks at Bob, blows the steam away, and takes a sip.

"There'll be enough when we're through."

McGredy lifts the small pot and slowly pours himself a cupful, inhaling the savory aroma. Drinking the warm liquid in front of Snarel seems to satisfy the gambler's vexed temper for the moment. The gaunt, pale-featured man watches them both through dark eyes and combs his fingers through his beard slowly.

"Whereabouts are you two headed?"

Elkman wipes the dampness from his mustache and pinches the tips at the corner of his mouth.

"North."

"How far?"

"A ways is all."

The three seem to sense the escalating tension between them as Snarel looks between Elkman and McGredy. He ignores McGredy's glare and turns back to Elkman.

"What ya headed north fer?"

McGredy blows into his steaming cup and gives a huff.

"Why you so interested?"

"Jest curious."

Taking a gulp of coffee, McGredy shakes his head as he swallows.

"For a fella who was just pulled out from the drink half-dead without his own blanket, you sure have some rude questions."

The dark eyes of Snarel snap over to McGredy and burn with a quiet intensity. He controls his temper and turns back to Elkman.

"No offense intended to either of yous. Jest curious 'bout the crowd I'm with is all."

McGredy grunts. "When we found ya, you didn't seem all that particular." Putting the tin cup to his lips, McGredy takes another sip and spitefully enjoys the scrawny man watching him drink the coffee. Bob Snarel licks his lips and glances down at his wrists.

"In my experience out here, you got to be some careful of who you ride with."

Elkman studies Snarel's gaze. "What experience might that be?"

Snarel fakes a smile. "I've just run in with some bad folks in the past is all."

McGredy takes a final sip and tosses out the last bit of coffee in his cup along with the dregs. He stands and stares down at Snarel, then turns to Elkman.

"Hell, we save his hide and he goes accusing us of bein' characters of ill repute. From the looks of him and his experiences, I'd rather not ride with his sort."

Snarel stares up at McGredy in hope that he will offer the use of his empty cup. McGredy makes a show of stepping over to his saddlebags and tucking his drinking vessel inside. He looks back toward the campfire and snorts.

"I usually have a pretty good nose for when trouble's about to follow. If he's gonna ride along with us, he needs to give a damned explanation."

Bob Snarel stands and drops the blanket from his shoulders. He glances to Elkman and takes a step toward McGredy. The frail man sticks out his meager chest and glares at McGredy.

"What are you getting at, *friend?*"

Elkman watches from under the brim of his hat as he pours the remainder of the coffee. Rising full height, McGredy puffs out the bulk of his shoulders, preparing for a fight.

"You looking to get walloped hard and thrown back in that river where you come from?"

The confrontation intensifies and Snarel, not wanting to back down from the challenge, takes another step toward McGredy. Almost amused, Elkman rises from his seat at the fire and stands between them. He passes his tin cup to Bob and puts his hand to McGredy's shoulder.

"Easy now . . . the both of you need to cool yer heels."

McGredy shakes his head as he looks past Elkman toward Snarel.

"I've seen rope burns like that b'fore and they weren't on no man I heard of that didn't deserve it. Now you explain what type of business you're dealing in or we'll drop yer ass right here for the Injuns to catch up with and finish off."

Snarel stares at McGredy a long minute then turns his attention toward Elkman.

"That how you feel too?"

The tension seems to quell for the moment as Elkman takes a step away from McGredy and gives a nod.

"I try my best not to waste my time with folks that can't steer a decent path."

Elkman looks to McGredy astutely and then back to Bob.

"If'n you want to continue on with us, you've some explaining to do."

The three stand in a circle around the campfire and study the others. Bob Snarel runs his tongue over his yellowed teeth and spits aside. He steps back to the blanket on the ground and picks it up. The gaunt man faces Elkman, squares his shoulders, and offers the borrowed covering.

"Your aid is appreciated, but my affair is none of yourn."

McGredy reaches out and snatches his blanket from Snarel. With a huff he stomps away and mumbles under his breath.

"Good. You're a damn liar anyhow. Glad to be rid of ya."

They both watch McGredy walk away and hear his talk plain. The fire snaps to life as Elkman nudges the embers with his boot and flames take to several of the unburned sticks. Elkman turns to Bob who raises the tin cup in a thankful salute.

The shadowy character of Bob Snarel moves away from the fireside to the edge of camp. Pulling up his torn, ratted shirt, Snarel eases back on a warming rock to watch the men stow their camp gear. He glares toward McGredy, watching him vigorously shake out his blanket and roll it. With sharp eyes that scan every detail before him, Snarel takes a sip from the coffee cup and murmurs low.

"We'll see who's rid of who . . ."

Chapter 9

Gear packed and mounted, Elkman and McGredy sit their horses across camp from the mysterious Bob Snarel. He still leans with his back against the large warm rock and watches, jaw set and eyes narrow. McGredy glances over at him momentarily then looks back at Elkman.

"You ready?"

"Yaugh, I'll be along shortly."

The two men exchange a nod and Elkman holds his mount back and waits while McGredy canters away. Elkman rides over and eases his horse up next to Bob. He looks down at him and they study each other a long silent moment. Elkman acknowledges Snarel's unspoken resolve for secrecy and gives the neck of his horse a pat.

"Good luck to ya then."

Snarel hands up the empty coffee cup and nods quietly. Elkman takes the metal cup and tucks it under the flap on his saddle bag. He nudges his animals forward and, without another word, follows after McGredy. A short distance away, Elkman steals a slight glance over his shoulder and observes the silhouetted form of Bob Snarel still set against the stone, watching them depart.

The day in the saddle wanes on as Elkman and McGredy move along single file through a rocky canyon. The calm, unmoving air hangs heavy and beads of perspiration run down from under the brims of their hats. They watch the ridge overhead and feel uneasiness at each blind turn of the craggy walls.

The water cut in the canyon widens the trail and Elkman holds back on the reins easing his saddle mount back alongside McGredy. He steers his pack animal to the opposite side and looks questioningly to the unusually quiet trail mate who stares forward.

"That was odd."

McGredy lifts in the stirrups, adjusting to get airflow beneath.

"Ne'er is much of a breeze in them slot canyons."

"Naw, I'm talkin' earlier."

The burly gambler continues his stare ahead with a perturbed glimpse over his shoulder.

"What?"

"You don't find it uneasy to save a life one day then jest leave it to die on another?"

McGredy turns to Elkman as he sits horseback beside him. He wipes the sweat beads that zig zags down his cheek and shrugs.

"He's a damn liar in my book, could see it plain. What he's running from or hiding at, he figures it's worth the risk. He chose it, not us."

Elkman gives a tug on the pack animal's lead rope as it drifts away and he nods his head in reluctant agreement.

"Yaugh . . . well, it don't seem right."

The two ride along silent for a while and McGredy shifts in his saddle, becoming uneasy. The light of afternoon sun shines high on the east wall of the canyon trail and slowly climbs higher. McGredy scans the top embankment of the rocky gorge and glances at Elkman.

"Suppose we'll ever run into him again?"

"If'n we do, he probably won't be too grateful toward either of us."

McGredy grins and cocks his head.

"Nope, don't expect he would be. That's gratitude for ya."

Elkman observes McGredy's strangely pleased attitude and continues the course of travel through the canyon.

From a distance, the Sugar Tooth Silver Mines have the appearance of a large ant colony. Paths crisscross along the side of the mountain leading to holes cut in the rock with trailings from diggings heaped and cascading down the grade.

In the shadowed valley below, a mixture of canvas and cut lumber forms a tent city. Elkman and McGredy crest the rise and look down at the mining camp. McGredy stands in the stirrups and peers into the valley.

"Hell, Tomas . . . looks as if there might be no less than a dozen watering holes down there."

"One is jest fine with me."

McGredy sits back against the saddle cantle and wipes his hand across his mouth.

"That's all I need, one at a time."

Elkman raises a wary eye toward McGredy and urges his horse forward down the graded trail.

"I ain't sure I left the right sort of trouble behind me."

McGredy sits and smiles a moment before realizing Elkman may not have paid him a compliment.

"Hey Tomas . . . whatchya mean by that?"

Elkman continues down the rocky path toward the tent city. He glances over his shoulder at McGredy and maneuvers his animals toward a livery barn on the outskirts of the bustling settlement. McGredy comes up from behind and rides alongside.

"Jest ta let you know, the kind of trouble I attract is all mostly good fun. Nothing like what ya get with that wet, half-runt Snarel fella with his sun blisters and staked wrists."

"Yeah?"

"Ya could jest tell that fella was trouble by his eyes."

"Sure."

"Well, you say *sure*, but I don't think ya mean it."

"Alright."

The stable owner steps out from the inside of the barn and tucks his hands high in his vest pockets. His short, skinny frame faces the two men on horseback.

"What kin I do ye fer?"

Elkman moves his horse up closer and dallies off the lead rope to his pack animal on his saddle horn. He leans down, peering into the shaded light of the shelter, and tips his hat back a bit.

"Lookin' for a place to stow gear and bed these animals down for the night."

The stableman eyes Elkman's two animals then turns a queried eye toward McGredy, who sits scratching his fingers through the whiskers under his beard around his neck.

"Him too?"

Elkman glances over at McGredy and nods.

"Yep."

"Four bits apiece for grain 'nd beddin'."

Hearing the mutual price, McGredy gets a bit ruffled and makes an obvious display of the vacant ground around his single horse.

"Four bits apiece? There's jest me atop this hay burner, and he's got two animals."

The stable owner nods, shifts the quid of tobacco in his cheek then spits a juicy stream of brown saliva.

"Yep, comes out 'bout right since he looks like he'll take care of his animals hisself. You'll need 'xtry attention."

His dander up a bit, McGredy eyes Elkman's amused audience and stares down at the livery man.

"It's yer job, sir."

"Yep, 'nd there's more of it with you."

Elkman dismounts and hands a few coins to the stableman.

"That's fine."

Still astride, McGredy digs in his vest, looks over his coinage and murmurs. "Damn robbery, tryin' to clean me out . . ."

He tosses the four bits to the skinny man who catches them midair in a surprisingly quick flash of movement. He feels the coins over with his finger in his open palm and nods.

"Foller me 'nd I'll show you where you kin bed down yer animals 'nd put yer gear. Fresh water yonder if'n yer needin' to git purdy some too."

McGredy dismounts and watches the stable owner scuffle down the center aisle inside the barn. Straw dust kicks up from the skinny man's dragging boot heels and he disappears into a glowing haze of afternoon sunshine. McGredy pats his vest.

"Rates like these sure do cut into my social and drinkin' funds. Don't leave much on the bone for female companionship."

Removing his hat, Elkman smiles as he rubs his forehead where the tanned hat-line reveals time in the outdoor elements. He runs his fingers along the damp insides of his felt hat and places it back on his head.

"He said he'll let you wash up in the horse water. Almost worth near the price of a bath."

McGredy eyes the long handled pump and the wooden trough near the corrals. He dismounts with a scowl and leads his horse to the barn, giving the bin of water a thumping kick as he walks past. McGredy hollers over his shoulder toward Elkman.

"I ain't paying for a bath in horse slobber."

Elkman follows to the barn with his animals. He smiles and gives the water in the horse trough a splash as he walks by.

Chapter 10

The afternoon rays of light dip low over the hills as Elkman and McGredy stroll along the main street in the tent city. McGredy sorts through the coins in his vest again and grunts.

"My funds are in need of bolsterin' since leavin' that last town in a haste. I've got some work to do."

"You mean gambling?"

McGredy gives Elkman a wry look.

"When I work, it ain't gamblin'."

"From what I've seen it ain't nearly honest either. I've ne'er seen someone handle a deck with so many face cards."

Elkman rubs his hand across his midsection.

"Yer welcome to do what you do but I'm fixin' to get a warm meal and ask around 'bout real work."

There is a clinking chime of coins as McGredy slides his seed money back into his vest.

"I don't cheat. Just some manipulatin' the order of the cards is sometimes needed for entertainment. That's a service worth something. You enjoyed losing to me a bit, right?"

Elkman thinks it over as he walks and raises an amused look.

"N'er heard it put that way, but you do have a spark for keeping the table lively."

McGredy grins as he marches along.

"Knew a fella once, back at one of them military forts, that claimed to be a magician of sorts. He was a hell of a card sharp. Them soldier boys lost a heap of money to him but had a hell of a good time doin' it."

"I'll keep that in mind the next time I sit at cards with ya."

McGredy adjusts his necktie and pats his vest with a smile.

"This lifestyle ain't cheap, but a card cheat will git shot and I ain't looking to get gunned down in no dingy saloon . . . dying in the arms of an angry woman is more my speed."

With his haughty strut, McGredy exudes the role of a gambling entertainer from all of his being. He looks to a group of dirt-caked miners walking toward them and steps aside gracefully so as not to get their filthiness on him.

"Ever do any mining, Tomas?"

"Nope. I don't believe the stale air would agree with me."

They turn from the main sewage-slopped street of the mining camp and eye the working types mingled about. Their dirty, mud-caked clothes make it hard to tell whether they are beginning or ending their shift in the ground.

The two resume their walk and climb up to the wood slab boardwalk. McGredy steps from the path of another group of particularly rough and dirty laborers and snorts.

"It's the work part of it that don't agree with me."

Standing along the walkway, Elkman smells the aroma of food and looks up at a sign: HOT VITTLES 'ND GRUB. He peers into the establishment and his empty insides start to rumble and churn.

"I'll sort up with you later."

McGredy half listens as he eyes the number of various saloons up and down the street. He wipes his hand across his whiskers and puts his fists to his hips to think on his gaming selection. Elkman moves to the door of the eatery and McGredy grins at him.

"Jest listen for a hoot-snortin' good time as yer walkin' down the street and I'll be there."

Elkman opens the door to the café and looks back.

"If I hear a ruckus, I'll figure you've found trouble 'nd git the other way quick."

McGredy tips his hat. "Fair 'nough."

He watches Elkman enter the eating establishment and continues down the plank walkway.

The cool air of evening has set in and the tent city glows with the illuminated hue of weather stained canvas. Elkman walks the main street smoking a shop-rolled cigar and observes his surroundings. He passes several tent saloons that emit the general clamor and racket from people drinking and having a good time.

Near the far end of the street, Elkman stops when he hears a familiar bellow from inside a high roofed canvas structure. He exhales a puff of smoke and pauses outside to listen.

"Come on ya sissies! There has to be one of you girls that can knock me off this mountain . . . I'll betcha a bottle of whiskey fer it . . . or a ginger ale if you please."

His curiosity piqued, Elkman steps to the doorway and takes a gander inside. Just shy of the entrance, Elkman looks around the wood-sided and canvas saloon. His jaw nearly drops from the sight of McGredy standing on the bar-top, high above the rest with a bottle of whiskey swinging in one hand and a ladies' peacock tail feather waving in the other.

A miner rushes the bar and McGredy greets him with a hard fist, the one holding the feather, to the jaw. Another miner grabs at his legs and McGredy does a little Irish jig and puts his boot-heel to the man's temple. With a snort of laughter, McGredy takes another swig of whiskey and sprays it out over the room.

Everyone ducks as the whiskey mist settles on the crowd. McGredy holds the bottle high and pours it into his mouth. He spots Elkman by the entrance and stops mid-gulp, still holding the yellowish-brown colored bottle high. Whiskey pours past his cheek, splashing off his shoulder as he calls out.

"Tomas H. Elkman, the most goodest man I recently knowed and ever had the pleasure of him being around me!"

Elkman runs his hand over his mustache to hide a grin, puts a finger to the brim of his hat and salutes. McGredy takes another swallow from the bottle and bellows across the room.

"Watch this Tomas! Them all have tried at least once. Now, here's a reward . . ."

Putting the long feather between his teeth, McGredy shuffles across the wooden bar-top and puts several small coins on the shiny nose of the buffalo shoulder mount. Through an unsteady and drunken haze he places the coins carefully and the room watches amused.

On the opposite end of the bar, a cowboy starts to creep up and makes it nearly top-side before McGredy notices. Roaring like an enraged bull with feather and bottle in hand, McGredy thunders down the wooden surface and slams his outstretched boot in the man's chest, sending him flying into the crowd. He swings out at another cowhand nearby and does a spin as his unchecked momentum carries him around. A tall, slender man emerges from the crowd, approaching the bar, and McGredy promptly smashes the whiskey bottle down on his head.

"Who will be the man enough to win the prize? Toss me another bottle!"

Surprisingly, someone in the crowd tosses a half-full bottle and McGredy snatches it from the air before it connects with his head, the intended target. McGredy laughs so hard, he nearly falls from his perch. With an amused tap of his cigar, Elkman turns and exits the establishment.

The firm grip of someone on his shoulder turns Elkman around and he instinctively puts his hand to the butt of his revolver. About to jerk his pistol, Elkman comes face to face with a bloody-mouthed, stout, bearded man wearing a barkeep's apron. The smashed nose and whimpering sadness in the man's eyes puts Elkman off guard and he relaxes his grip on his sidearm.

"Can I help ya?"

The bearded man removes his hand from Elkman's shoulder and wipes his face, smearing the free-flowing blood from his nose.

"Yes, sir. I own this here establishment and if'n you know this feller, I'd appreciate it if you git him to leave 'fore I don't have any whiskey or customers left."

Elkman peers around the stout man as McGredy charges across the bar and violently clobbers another man with his fist.

"I don't know him that well."

He turns to leave and the battered saloon owner takes a grab at his shoulder again. Elkman turns back slowly and glares at the blood-smeared hand still holding on his vest.

"You won't be doing that again, sir."

The man pulls his hand away quick with apologies.

"I'm sorry mister but I got to get that feller out of my place while I still have one to claim."

"That's none of my concern."

"I'll pay ye."

"Jest to git him out of there?"

The saloon owner digs in his apron pocket and pulls out two California gold pieces. He looks up at Elkman pleading.

"No one can git close to the bar, or that side of the room for that matter, without his head gettin' pushed in."

The saloon owner holds out the coins in offering.

Elkman looks at the money, then at McGredy trying to swing like an oversized ape over the bar on one of the hanging kerosene chandeliers. Without further thought, Elkman scoops up the two gold pieces and tucks them in his upper vest pocket. He nods and looks inside again. "Alright, I'll see what I kin do."

Several patrons move aside as Elkman carefully maneuvers through the crowd. He steps around random men on the sawdust floor holding bloody noses and injured limbs. He approaches the bar, hooks his boot heel on the rail and looks up.

"Hey ya big bully, this yer idea of fun?"

McGredy stomps over and smiles down at Elkman.

"Yeahhh . . ."

His attention distracted to the opposite end of the saloon, McGredy spots another cowboy bellying up to the bar-top.

"Hold this, be right back!"

McGredy shoves the bottle of whiskey into Elkman's hands then charges down to greet the challenger. Seeing McGredy coming toward him, the cowboy leaps from the slab and lands on a table surrounded by a cluster of occupied chairs.

Elkman reaches behind the bar and grabs himself a glass tumbler. He pours from McGredy's bottle and lifts it to his mouth. Before the drink reaches his lips, McGredy swipes it from his hand and tosses it back through his own whiskey soaked chin-whiskers. Up on the bar-top, squatting down on his haunches, McGredy wipes his mouth satisfied and grins widely at Elkman.

"What brings you down to these parts?"

He laughs rousingly at his own drunken humor and slaps his hand heavily on Elkman's shoulder.

Elkman turns his gaze to McGredy's hand on his vest the same place the barkeep grasped at him and grabs another glass. He pours himself a second drink and raises his eyes to McGredy squatted before him.

"Where's yer feather?"

McGredy looks quizzically at his empty hand on Elkman's vest and shrugs. Elkman rolls his shoulder.

"I come to git you down from there. Your horse misses you and sent me lookin' for ya."

The commotion in the bar continues as McGredy leans on Elkman for support. He eyes several men as they contemplate taking the bar-top challenge. The intoxicated gambler is quiet a moment as he thinks over Elkman's statement then breaks into uncontrolled giggles, then laughter.

"Let the old nag wait!"

He throws the shot-glass across the room, shattering it on one of the wooden upright supports and grabs the bottle from Elkman's hand. He takes a swig, does a jig, and takes another swallow. McGredy laughs as he pours the bottle in his mouth again and sprays the onlookers with a shower of whiskey.

"I'm not leaving until I get dragged from this bar."

Elkman reaches up and grabs the near empty bottle from McGredy as he swings it past while charging across the wooden slab of a bar.

The room is an unruly chaos as Elkman studies the situation. He shakes his head and pours the amber liquid from the bottle, filling his glass halfway and emptying the glass container.

"Yer choice . . ."

As McGredy dances down the bar, Elkman looks to the empty bottle in hand. He takes a sip from the glass and leans back as the heavy-booted gambler shuffles by in a high-prancing raucous hop. After he passes again, Elkman reaches out and lays the empty bottle on its rounded side in McGredy's return path.

The boisterous gambler pounds the wood bar, rattling the glass bar-back and making the slab flex under his weight.

"Hee lew! Skip to my Lou . . ."

McGredy jumps in a dancing high-step and lands on alternating feet. He does a backward shuffle and hits the rolling bottle with a whiskey-slicked boot heel.

In a flash, both feet are mid-air and McGredy comes crashing down on his back. A thunderous crack is heard as his skull connects with the liquor-soaked wood. Elkman finishes his drink and sets the glass down next to the dazed McGredy.

There is a mad rush to the area as several men grab McGredy's arms and legs and drag him from his perch. Elkman steps away and leads the escorts toward the entryway.

"This a'way boys. Toss 'em outside."

Everyone is quickly pushed aside as the porters charge past and toss the stunned McGredy out on his head. Elkman steps into the cool night air while the men pat each other on the back, laughing and reentering the tent structure. The saloon owner steps out, looks at Elkman, and tosses McGredy's hat to the street.

The sounds of the drinking establishment return to normal business and Elkman looks down the dark, dirt-rutted road. He walks over to McGredy still sprawled out and nudges him with the toe of his boot.

"You alive yet?"

The big man rolls over and stares up drunkenly at Elkman. He grins and gives a giggle.

"Wasn't sure how I was going to git out of that one."

"Hell of an exit plan."

McGredy sits up and wipes dirt from his face.

"But it was fun warn't it?"

"C'mon, git up. I'm not dragging your big carcass down the street."

Elkman helps pull McGredy to his feet and the drunken rabble-rouser nearly falls again when he leans down to pick up his hat.

With the labored help from Elkman, the two stumble down the empty street under the occasional glowing oil lamp outside a canvas building. McGredy stops a moment and leans forward, resting his hands to his knees. Elkman pauses and waits as the drunken man takes slow, deep, sobering breaths. McGredy looks up at Elkman, holds up a finger, and gives a half-sauced grin.

"Hold it a minute, something's a brewin'."

"You okay . . . gonna make it?"

The large man spits to the side and takes another heaving breath.

"What happened in there? I thought I was doing fine."

Elkman pulls a hand-rolled cigar from his vest and chews the end off. He lights a match and the flare brightens his amused expression.

"You fell off the bar."

"Really? I don't remember that . . ."

Elkman touches the flame to his cigar and inhales a few puffs.

"That's what happened."

McGredy touches the back of his head gingerly and shrugs. He slowly stands upright and continues down the street toward the livery stable. Walking a few paces together, McGredy looks over at Elkman questioningly.

"Tomas?"

"Yeah?"

"My horse really say she missed me?"

Elkman blows out a ring of smoke and nods.

"Yep."

McGredy snorts through his nose and stumbles on.

"Hah . . . I knew it."

Chapter 11

The town is quiet in the predawn hours with the exception of livery animals eating their morning meal. A cold mountain chill hangs in the air as Elkman steps outside the livery barn, wrapped in his coat, and watches the empty street. The occasional miner crosses the spaces between, from one tent structure to another, but the drinking and cavorting from the prior night has settled. Gray trickles of smoke start to drift skyward from long metal stacks protruding from canvas-covered rooftops.

Hands deep in his pockets, Elkman watches from under the broad brim of his hat and scans the dugout hills and untouched mountains beyond. He is absorbed in the quiet of daybreak and enjoys the pleasures of the peaceful sunrise through his stillness. A bird flutters overhead as Elkman watches the faint mist of his exhaled breath. His nose twitches, which brings his hand out to brush down unruly mustache whiskers that curl and touch his nostril. Running his tongue across the smooth front of his teeth, he takes out his fixings and begins to make a smoke.

A groan and scuffle of boots in gravel catches his attention and Elkman looks to the wide barn entrance. McGredy steps into the long beam of early light that reaches over the hills and squints painfully.

Bedecked with random bits of straw stuck in his hair and beard, he puts both hands to his temples.

"What happened last night?"

Elkman strikes a match to light the hand-rolled, glances down the empty path through town, and sniffs, amused.

"What do you remember happen'n?"

The throbbing pain of the prior evening's events causes McGredy to wince and lean on the door to the barn. He drags his feet over to the wooden water trough and gingerly sits on the front edge, peering down at his reflection. McGredy evaluates his rumpled clothing and picks pieces of straw from his vest.

"I did some gamblin' then went to do some drinkin'."

Elkman stamps the cold from his feet and stretches.

"Sounds 'bout right."

He drops the spent match to the ground between his boots and smothers it. After a few puffs on the tobacco, Elkman tosses it aside and lets a waif of smoke escape his lips. He takes a last look at the peaceful mining town and moves past McGredy, stepping inside the barn. Elkman grabs his headstall and lead rope and goes to work. McGredy watches in a daze as Elkman leads his pack animal from the corral and begins to load his gear.

"Where you off to this early, cowboy . . . what time is it?"

"Daytime."

Elkman continues with the pack saddle and ties on his canvas paniers. The animal lazily rubs his face on the nearby wood support as the light load is fastened. With his possessions secure, Elkman grabs his bit and bridle from a wall peg and enters his horse's stall.

McGredy massages his face all over to wake himself and attempts to smooth down his beard. He saunters inside the barn and leans on the pack animal's rump as Elkman leads his riding horse out from the barn stall.

"You leaving?"

"No horseback work for me here. The ranches east of here might be hiring though. You'd might want to pack it up as well."

The pack animal swishes its tail and McGredy grabs a hold of the end. He twirls and braids the coarse hair aimlessly.

"Why's that?"

Glancing over his shoulder, Elkman appears a little surprised.

"You don't remember too much of last night?"

"Nope . . . not much."

McGredy pats his vest pocket and feels for his money stash.

"Appears I did quite well at the tables though."

Elkman finishes brushing his horse and runs his hand under the belly to feel for smoothness. He drops the brush in a wooden pail and grabs his saddle blanket from the top of his saddle on the stable door. He looks back at McGredy and gives the blanket a slight shake.

"When you git to drinkin' you tend to upset folks."

McGredy watches as Elkman slides the blanket on the horses back and smooths it behind the withers. Still aching in the head, McGredy drops the pack animal's tail and dusts himself off again.

"Don't remember anything in particular, but suppose you're right."

He peeks down again into his vest pocket and grins to himself.

"There might be a feller or possibly two sore at me for taking some of their earnings."

"And other things."

McGredy looks up at Elkman, pats his vest pocket, reflects a moment, and starts for his horse's stall.

"There were other things . . . ?"

Elkman lifts his slick fork saddle, gives it a jiggle to settle the rigging and tosses it over the blanketed mount.

"Yep."

"Anyone get hurt?"

Elkman shrugs. "Nothin' permanent."

McGredy leads his horse out and runs his hand quick over the animals back before tossing the blanket on. He throws his saddle over the blanket and peers over the smooth leather seat at Elkman as he tightens the cinch.

"You mind if'n I keep on with ya 'nother day or so?"

"It's a free country."

"That's good to hear. If'n it was anythin' too serious, you'd have skedaddled already."

Elkman raises his booted foot and puts it to the stirrup. With a natural ease, he swings into the saddle and adjusts his coat around the high cantle seat. He presses his leg to the mount's midsection and side steps his horse across to the waiting pack animal. After untying the lead rope and coiling it in hand, Elkman looks down at McGredy.

"Best not to forget we ain't riding together permanent. . . . Only till I find work."

McGredy ties on his blanket over his saddle bags and leads his horse outside after Elkman.

"Sure thing, Tomas. I won't be sticking around anyone trying to do an honest day's work. . . . Makes me some ill jest to think about it."

Elkman stands his animals and waits as McGredy climbs into the saddle and starts to walk his horse toward the path leading through town.

"Jefferson . . ."

Turning in the saddle and wincing from the throbbing at the back of his skull, McGredy looks back questioningly.

"No?"

"It'd probably be best if we went around."

McGredy gingerly pushes up his hat and touches the lump on the back of his head. He turns his horse and rides past Elkman toward the hills and gives a feeble smile.

"That bad, huh?"

Elkman nods and gives his horse a prod. The two ascend the rising trail out of the mined valley, leaving the tent city in an early morning haze of wood smoke and quiet below.

Through the high country of pines and rocky trails, Elkman and McGredy travel in a single-file line. The trail widens some after a turn and Elkman checks behind at McGredy to observe on his condition. The hungover gambler still looks ill at ease while trying to shake off his throbbing headache. McGredy puts spur to hide and trots up next to Elkman. He looks to the surrounding countryside, removes his hat, and lays it over his saddle horn. Touching the back of his head delicately, McGredy winces at the sharp pain.

"Head hurts like I was hit with a club."

Elkman glances over at him.

"Guess it was the whiskey."

McGredy continues to rub the lump on the back of his head.

"No, I mean I've got a headache 'nd all, but this spot on my noggin' hurts like I was hit with something."

The trail flattens out ahead and Elkman eases his horse to a faster walking pace. He turns to McGredy with mock concern and shrugs innocently.

"Hmm. Wonder what happened?"

Elkman taps his open palm on his vest pocket where two gold coins clink inside and continues on while McGredy runs his fingers through the hair over the raised swelling.

"Cripes, me too."

The big man lifts his hat and adjusts it on his head painfully then peers back over his shoulder at the lingering smoke from the tent city in the far distance. Elkman rides the trail ahead following the mountain path into the high country before them.

Chapter 12

Elkman and McGredy ride silently along, listening to the gentle sounds of horse hooves on stones with the occasional crack of a broken stick or rustle of leaves. They move alongside the other, surrounded by rocky boulders in the broken shade of tall, thin aspen trees. McGredy rides easy and content, then stops and scans the area. He studies the sun through the trees and looks around to get his bearings. "Hey rein up a bit?"

Elkman turns his head slightly and continues riding.

"Hold up there Tomas, I think we might be headed wrong."

"How's that?"

"We look to be goin' a ways south."

"Yep."

Confused, McGredy prods his horse, catches up, and rides with Elkman. "Where are we going?"

"I'm headed for Kishwaukee Valley."

"Is that a boom town?"

Elkman shakes his head to the negative and adjusts his hat.

"Nope, jest a place."

"What kinder place?"

"A rancher near there was said to be paying good wages to git a passel of horses escorted north."

McGredy's ears perk at the mention of money.

"That's some good luck. We both can make a tidy sum on the way up north."

Elkman continues on silently and McGredy rides alongside. He thinks a moment and looks to Elkman questioningly.

"How's it you're just mentioning it to me now?"

"I didn't mention it . . . you asked."

"When were you plannin' on tellin' me?"

Elkman glances over. "Wasn't certain you'd make it out of that camp without riding the rail in tar 'nd feathers."

In an effort to hide a smile, McGredy looks away and pats his money-eyed vest pocket. He keeps his horse paced with Elkman and gestures matter-of-factly.

"You should have told me anyways, us being almost, nearly partners 'nd such?"

Sensing McGredy's teasing charm, Elkman tries to resist the bait.

"We ain't partners."

The big gambler reaches out and gives Elkman a pat on the arm.

"Well you could say riding companions then."

"We may share the same trail 'nd that's fine but when the chips fall and fellers get to dancin' on the bar, I only take care of me and my own."

McGredy touches the lump on the back of his head suspiciously and gets a queer expression on his face.

"Who's dancin' on the bar?"

"I've seen it happen with some."

McGredy nods and shrugs the foggy visualization off.

"Kinder a lonely attitude for ya, ain't it?"

Elkman stares ahead and continues riding.

"Like I said . . . I ain't asked you to ride along."

McGredy slows back a few paces and snorts, bemused. He leans down on his saddle horn, takes out a folding knife along with a stick of chewing tobacco, and cuts off a piece of chaw. Placing it in his cheek, he wraps the remainder and places it back in his coat pocket. "Well, that's jest fine. Least I know where you stand."

Elkman calls out over his shoulder as he continues on.

"Jest layin' it to ya square."

Watching Elkman ride ahead leading the pack animal, McGredy looks to the lonely surroundings, tucks his knife away, and follows.

"Well, you's just one kick away from no company a'tall."

The light of evening sets in as Elkman pulls his boots off and lounges on his bedroll near the campfire. He watches as McGredy adds more gathered wood and pokes the flames, sending sparks into the darkening sky. McGredy looks over at him and scratches under his arm where his vest meets his shirt.

"How far is this place we're goin'?"

"Should be there tomorrow."

"You sure there ain't a town?"

"Could be some sort of settlement."

"How big?"

"Don't know, didn't ask."

McGredy sits back on his haunches, looks to the fire, and pokes it again. He thinks quietly to himself, then speaks.

"What's the feller's name yer lookin' for?"

"Not sure."

"How ya supposed to find 'em?"

"Guess I'll just look around some till I do."

"That work for you in the past?"

"Yep."

"Hmph . . . I always gone town to town, without lookin' around much in between. You ain't a fan of civilization are ye?"

Elkman turns away from the fire and looks skyward. He mumbles to himself under his breath. "I remember now the reason I didn't tell you about it."

Eyes heavy, Elkman relaxes into the quiet sounds of night and smell of the warming fire. With a grunt, McGredy stabs his stick into the flame and near whispers.

"Just curious what you got me into."

Elkman sits up on his bedroll and irritably turns toward McGredy.

"I didn't get you into anything!"

"No?"

"The only reason you're still along is ya can't stand *not* bein' social. Every place we been, you go 'nd make some sort of trouble, 'nd heck, ya talk more'n any fella I've ever come across."

McGredy giggles while he jabs the burning poker a few more times, lighting up the flames.

"Easy there, no reason to git cross or personal. I was jest testin' if you was still listenin'."

Annoyed but calmed, Elkman stares at McGredy a moment then lies back with his head against the seat of his saddle. He raises his hat over his face about to cover it and grunts.

"Any more questions?"

"None that I don't know your answer already."

Elkman sighs and hides his face under the brim.

"Good night."

"One more thing . . ."

Elkman turns away with his back to the fire and pulls up his blanket, moving his hat over the side of his head.

"I'm already asleep, McGredy."

The dark evening shadows of the trees rustle overhead as McGredy smiles to himself, amused. He continues to poke the fire and the glowing embers flicker and travel skyward while the sounds of nocturnal wildlife emanate from the darkness.

Chapter 13

In the south central regions of the Colorado Territory, the plains from the east come up against the mountainous foothills rising along the divide. At the base of the tree-lined hills, two riders and a pack animal crest the horizon and look down into a bustling basin filled with wooden buildings inhabited by saloons, gambling dens, and houses of ill repute.

At the edge of town, Elkman and McGredy steer their horses past wood-framed structures. McGredy smiles inwardly, satisfied with the town's apparent zeal for social drinking and lively entertainment.

"About time we run into a real town. I didn't seem to reach my potential for earnin's in that last tent-ditch-hovel and got an awful lump on my noggin ta boot."

Elkman shakes his head knowingly and snaps a finger against his vest pocket tapping the two gold coins.

"Lost it dancin' on the bar, 'spect."

McGredy looks over at Elkman, curious.

"What's that you say?"

"Jest keep to yerself till I find this horse-stock feller."

The two ride through town, looking over the active urban lifestyle. McGredy pats the trail dust from the shoulder of his topcoat.

"I don't go lookin' for trouble."

"Suppose it jest finds ya without much doin' on yer part?"

"Somethin' like that."

"Well, watch out for yerself."

"Oh that's right, or you'll jest leave me."

Elkman gives a shrug and steers his horse to a hitching rail at the side of the busy hard-packed earthen street.

"Yer free to go yer own way, I'm gonna get some vittles."

Still perched high in the saddle observing the busyness all around, McGredy steers his horse next to Elkman and brushes the remaining trail dirt from other parts of his clothing.

"I think I will join you if I'm not too much trouble."

The two exchange a humorous glance and dismount to tie their animals off, away from the flow of commerce in the street.

Seated at a table near the front of the room, Elkman and McGredy ingest and imbibe full plates of food and frothy mugs of beer. The dim room is lit only by a beam of sunlight streaming in through the door that reaches half across the room. Several tables occupy the establishment, but only a few customers dwell along the long stretch of bar. Elkman and McGredy quietly focus on the task at hand as they eat and delight in the warm cooked meal.

Outside, the sun drops on the horizon and the tumult of trade continues in the street. McGredy wipes his tin plate with a half-devoured piece of bread and cleans his chin and lip whiskers with his sleeve.

"What you got planned for the evening?"

Elkman lifts his mug and takes a swallow. He sets the glass of beer aside and quietly resumes his meal. He chews a mouthful unhurried and looks up at McGredy.

"I'm gonna see what I can find about that feller and those horses for takin' north."

"Hell, that won't take all night."

"Probably not."

"This burg is ripe for the picking."

McGredy watches as Elkman lifts his beer glass and takes another drink. He gives him a moment then pats his palms on the tabletop excitedly. "Let's find us a card game!"

Slowly setting down his drink, Elkman swipes his fingers across his mustache to clear the foamy bits. "I'll pass."

McGredy grunts, irritated, and fidgets in his seat.

"I know, I know . . . last time we sat at the cards I got you in a mess of trouble."

Elkman peers up at McGredy who laughs from across the table.

"Why you laughing? You did."

"What're the odds of somethin' like that happening again?"

McGredy sits straight and puts on an angelic posture.

"I'll be on my best behavior."

Elkman takes a deep breath and scrapes together the last mouthful from his plate. He finishes chewing his meal and sits back in the creaky wooden chair.

"Alright, a few hands would be alright."

With eyes bright and a playful smile, McGredy raises his beer mug in a salute and downs the remainder in one long gulp. He puffs out his chest and lets out a low grumbling belch that vibrates across the table. Elkman shakes his head unimpressed and McGredy slaps his palm across his lap.

"Good man, Tomas! I'm gonna show you a fun time at the tables tonight!"

The cards go around the table at the back of the room and Elkman sits opposite McGredy with another cowboy and miner taking dealt hands. Several bets are placed and Elkman lays out a winning hand. McGredy seems pleased with himself as Elkman pulls in the cash money. The big gambler grins broadly as he takes up the deck for another deal. "For a man who seldom plays, ye sure are cleaning up tonight."

Elkman looks to McGredy and studies him in short glances as he sorts his winnings. "Takes the pressure off when you ain't trying to make a living at it."

The other players at the table look to their meager spoils and watch as McGredy shuffles the cards and deals another hand. Elkman's eyes pass around the table and he catches the slightest of winks from the big gambler. Eagerly, McGredy tosses Elkman his third card and grins.

"Hell, you set at the cards like you're playing with someone else's money."

They all watch as the cards sling out to the players and Elkman curiously picks up his hand. McGredy slaps the dealer's deck on the table and smiles all around. With whimsical flare, McGredy roars across the room.

"Even losing is more enjoyable than an honest day's work."

The others at the table nod amiably and ante up. Elkman thumbs through his cards and glances up at McGredy suspiciously. He looks down at his pile of winnings and chews his bottom lip.

"I'm out. Looks as if my good fortune is done here."

McGredy looks across the table, surprised as Elkman folds his hand and slides his cards across the table. McGredy seems taken aback, almost shocked.

"Ain't much of a hand?"

"Not one I'm interested in."

"Sticking around for another?"

"Nope, I like to sleep well at night."

Elkman finishes his beer, collects his money and tips his hat as he pushes his chair back to stand.

"Good-night fellas."

McGredy thumbs through his card hand and looks sheepishly up at Elkman. The two exchange a knowing look that escapes the notice of the others.

"Maybe I kin get some of them good cards now."

"I have no doubt."

As Elkman walks to the door, several recreational women advance on him, vying for business. McGredy laughs and gestures to the continuing players at the table.

"Thing I love 'bout women is their aspiration for wealth."

Amused, McGredy watches his saddle pal politely excuse himself while easing out the front door. He antes up, deals to the others replacing their discards, and removes two from his own hand. McGredy draws two fresh cards and looks to his playing hand.

"Looks like my luck is changing already."

Chapter 14

The sign over the door reads Madame Tucks' Bordello in fancy, bright red lettering. The curtains on the window shimmer in the early morning sun as the front door opens and the sweet aroma of lilac waifs out. Elkman steps onto the wooden boardwalk and emerges from the establishment with an air of invigoration. He stands looking out to the street a moment before turning and admiring his reflection in the sun glinted window.

The scarf bandana at his neck flutters in the breeze and he twists it around to bring the slide knot to the front. The warmth of the morning light enlivens him and Elkman puffs up his chest and wipes his fingers across his mustache. Other than his unaffected hat, his cleaned clothing and shaved cheeks put an extra spring in his step as he moves down the plank walkway. With the faint scent of perfume following him, Elkman's eyes twinkle as he observes the already active street. He peers into one cafe, looking for McGredy, and moves on down the line of businesses.

Returning to the Benchwood Saloon, Elkman glances into the dim room from the prior night's card game. He lets his eyes wander down the bar a moment before moving on. The familiar grunt from an oversized gambler catches his attention and he turns back, strangely curious.

Elkman enters the saloon, sniffs the smell of stale tobacco smoke and lets his eyes adjust to the low light. He walks to the back of the establishment where four rough-looking characters sit crowded around the card table with McGredy.

"Morning boys, how's the game going?"

The card-players silently pause to stare at Elkman while McGredy looks up apologetically. "Morning . . ."

On quick observation of the table, Elkman notices McGredy's luck has much improved from the previous night. Most of the money in the game sits in front of the gambler yet unsuspected of questionable card dealings.

"Looks to be an interestin' game."

One of the card-players spits across the room toward the spittoon and the wad of chaw spittle splats to the wall. The man wipes his whiskered chin as the offensive sputum slowly rolls down the wood paneling to the floor.

"Table's full, beat it."

McGredy peers meekly up at his saddle pal and sniffs the air inquisitively at the hint of perfume. Elkman looks around to the unfriendly faces staring back at him and tips his hat graciously.

"Sorry to bother y'all."

An almost audible gulp is heard and McGredy looks crestfallen. He watches despairingly as Elkman turns on his heels and marches toward the front door. He half rises from his chair and the others around the table glare at him.

"Excuse me there, sir!"

Slowly, Elkman stops and turns.

"Who . . . me?"

McGredy smiles sheepishly.

"Could you do me a service?"

Elkman pats his vest pocket with an empty thump where his two gold coins were previously.

"Suppose'n I could if you're willin' to pay fer it."

Everyone looks to the largest pile of winnings as McGredy selects a few bills from his bounty and holds them out to Elkman.

"Could you get me some breakfast or some kind of eats? I've been here quite a while."

Elkman looks to the barkeep half-asleep leaning behind the bar with his head on his hands. The man looks up and shrugs then turns to stare back out the window. The room hangs quiet in suspense until Elkman frowns and walks back to the table. He peers down at the rascally card-handler and the tough spot he's put himself in. McGredy smiles up at Elkman with a pleading charm in his eyes.

"I'm so hungry I could eat a *horse.* Could you see what you could put together?" McGredy holds out several money bills and Elkman nods his head toward the pile of loot spread before him.

"Give me some of that silver too for my own breakfast."

McGredy looks at his pile and grins.

"Okay, but make it fast."

He snaps up a few coins and puts them in Elkman's hand. They both flinch when one of the players pounds his fist on the table.

"Ye ain't gonna spend that much of our money on fixin's!"

The oldest of the four, Boss Carloff leans forward, hiding his cards in his large sausage-fingered paw.

"Hold it . . ."

He stares at McGredy then looks up to Elkman. He reaches out and gently pulls a bill from McGredy's mitt.

"Jest get him half a horse to eat. His luck is about to change and I hate to waste a good meal on him."

With a nod, Elkman takes the rest of the bills and walks away, listening as the four men laugh uproariously back at the table. The sound of cards shuffling is the last thing he hears before he exits the saloon and slips the money in his vest pocket.

An occasional form passes the saloon double doors and McGredy watches for any type of diversion. He holds his cards cautiously and looks to the four unfriendly players opposite him at the table. He lays down his hand and winces. The card-players all stare at him menacingly as he rakes in the winnings again. Boss Carloff shakes his head and tips his hat back a smidge.

"I wouldn't advise ye to keep playing like that."

McGredy shrugs and stacks his winnings.

"I couldn't play this well if I tried."

"What do ya mean by that?"

One of the other card-players looks to his meager pile of cash and looks to McGredy's abundance of wealth.

"Why don't we just take our money back?"

Carloff looks around the table at his men.

"That'd be stealing."

McGredy forces a smile and looks to the front entrance in hopes for rescue. Stacking his paper money and coins, he squirms uneasy in his chair.

"I've really got to git going."

He makes a move to stand and Boss Carloff pulls his pistol and sets it on the table, quick but firm.

"Sit down McGredy. You ain't had yer breakfast yet."

McGredy slowly sinks into his chair and watches as the cards are dealt around. He takes up his hand and lets out a faint grunt as he holds a pair of Jacks. Keeping one eye on the door attentively, a shadowed figure finally appears. Blocking the incoming haze of morning light, one of the card-players looks over his shoulder and grumbles.

"Looks like yer last meal is here."

The backlit individual enters and walks the length of the room with a plate of food in hand. In what seems an eternity, Elkman finally stands over McGredy and sets the meal before him.

McGredy stares down at the plate of grits, sausage, and biscuits feeling a chilling wave of disappointment. He looks up at Elkman for some sort of liberation from his predicament and raises an eyebrow inquiringly.

"Thanks . . . ? Keep the change."

"Sure, glad to."

Elkman mockingly pats his vest pocket and turns to walk away. He feels McGredy's pleading eyes on him as he strides toward the door and pauses when he reaches the threshold.

Clenching his jaw, Elkman holds his step and tries to refrain from turning back to the table. He puts his hand to his hip and instinctively passes it over the worn walnut grip of his pistol. Lowering his gaze and taking a breath, Elkman listens as Boss Carloff speaks out with a rumbling growl.

"Eat yer damn grits McGredy and play them cards. We ain't gonna tolerate you winnin' another of these hands."

Glancing back, Elkman watches McGredy sitting dejected at the table. He turns and takes a few steps back toward the card game.

"Eh? Did I hear said, yer name's McGredy?"

McGredy looks up momentarily relieved.

"That's me, what of it?"

"There's a feller across the street lookin' for you."

McGredy leans to peer outside but seems confused.

"Who is it?"

Throwing a sarcastic look, Elkman tips his head toward the door. McGredy finally catches the hint and starts to pocket his money.

"I have to be going . . ."

Carloff puts his hand over the pistol on the table, rotating it toward McGredy as he cocks it.

"Sit down McGredy. Ye ain't going anywheres."

There is a long silence until another click of a pistol hammer being pulled back is heard. Boss Carloff slowly eases off his grip on the gun and spreads his hands out before him on the table. The men seated around the cards turn to see Elkman with his long barreled revolver resting on their boss's shoulder. Elkman stares down each man seated and nuzzles the front blade-sight of his pistol into Carloff's neck.

"Hate to turn this game unfriendly but ye best let this man see to his business."

McGredy smiles and grabs for the pot in the center of the table. In a subtle maneuver, Elkman thrusts the toe of his boot out, giving McGredy's chair a swift kick.

"Best leave that alone and be happy with what ye got."

Looking up at Elkman dismayed, McGredy slowly pulls his hands away from the cash on the table and lets the pot lay. He gathers the bills and coins before him and tucks them in his vest.

The card-player to McGredy's right suddenly scoots his chair back and reveals his holstered pistol.

"Yer not leaving with my money!"

McGredy quickly swings out, knocking the man's hat back and grabbing him by the forelock of his hair. Before the card-player can jerk his pistol, the swift-handed gambler pulls the man's head down and slams his face into the tabletop. McGredy lets him up to reveal a flattened nose with a trickle of blood smeared to the side.

Gesturing with his pistol, Elkman angrily waves McGredy toward the door.

"Git yerself outside!"

He motions the pistol toward the other card-players and steps back.

"You fellers best keep comfortable in them seats for a bit."

McGredy rises and gives a salutation of his hat to the others at the table as he walks toward the street exit. Backing away slowly, Elkman follows with his gun still raised and then holsters it as he steps through the door.

Outside, seeing his horse tied and saddled, McGredy turns and smiles to Elkman. Unexpectedly, a fist slams into McGredy's jaw, spinning him to the boardwalk. He looks up questioningly to see the infuriated face of his liberator. McGredy rubs his bearded chin and winces.

"What the hell's matter with you?" Elkman rubs his clenched fingers and moves to his tied animals.

"If'n yer coming, ya best pick yerself up."

Climbing to his feet, McGredy touches the inside of his busted lip. "Damn..."

McGredy watches Elkman step into the saddle and looks inside the saloon window toward the back of the room. He sees the gang all gathered around the man with the smashed nose and he smiles, satisfied. When they notice him watching at the window, they all start toward the door.

Elkman backs his horse away from the hitching rail and starts down the street. His pack animal balks and Elkman jerks the leading rope tight. "Ye coming or not?"

Boots scuffling, McGredy leaps from the boardwalk and climbs into the saddle. "Yes, sir!"

His horse backed away from the hitching rail, McGredy turns his mount broadside to the saloon entrance and holds the animal in a prancing jig. He waits until the men appear at the double doors and then lets his horse leap forward.

Elkman trots down the street and McGredy follows at an easy lope. The gambler turns back toward the saloon and gives a waving salute toward the angry gang assembled at the front of the building. The men stand and scowl, unable to pursue their lost plunder.

As the two horseback men ride down the main street of town at a fast trot, Elkman notices a familiar face watching him from between buildings. He turns to take a second look and the appearance is gone. At the end of the street, he feels a strange uneasiness and urges his mounts to a faster pace.

With the town at a safe distance behind them, McGredy catches up and slows his horse to a trotting walk. He rides alongside Elkman and grins.

"Didn't think you'd come through for me back there."

Elkman rides along without acknowledging McGredy and the thankful gambler continues talking regardless.

"Hell, when you brought that food plate in for me I thought I was done fer good."

McGredy paces along with Elkman but gets no response.

"The way you acted back there . . . I thought you were goin' to leave me to them mangy dogs."

Turning toward McGredy with a solemn expression, Elkman nods then finally cracks a grin.

"I was."

McGredy's brow drops and he rides along quietly a moment.

"Yer not kidding, are ya?"

Elkman taps his spurs to his mount and rides on ahead. Touching his bloody lip, McGredy grunts and urges his mount forward to catch Elkman in the lead.

"Well, all's square now. What's yer hurry?"

"I thought I saw someone back there."

"Who?"

Elkman glances at McGredy as they ride alongside each other.

"Yer pal, Snarel."

McGredy thinks a moment and seems stunned.

"That feller Bob . . . really? Did he see you?"

"Maybe."

McGredy lets his horse slow and looks self-consciously over his shoulder toward the town just absconded from.

"Damn . . . that'd be some bad luck."

The pack animal lags behind and Elkman gives the lead rope a tug.

He glances back at McGredy watching the back-trail and rides on.

Chapter 15

A lush, grass-filled valley spreads out from the landscape and several dozen horses graze peacefully in the mid-day sun. Elkman and McGredy look out over the horse operation and see the ranch house of Henry Martin in the distance surrounded by barns and corrals. McGredy leans an elbow down on his saddle horn and whistles low.

"Holy cripes. . . . This is a hell of a nice setup."

Elkman lets his eyes travel over the picturesque setting.

"This is the kinder spread that ya never let go."

McGredy nods and lets the view settle upon him.

"If'n I was a workin' man, this is the kind of place I would settle down for sure."

"But you ain't, huh?"

"No, sir."

Elkman smiles and adjusts the split leather reins of his mount between his fingers. He dangles the loose ends absentmindedly and admires the view of the ranch.

"Well, it would take a bit more'n a handsome view for me to want to settle in one place for too long."

"A gold mine or two would help."

Elkman grins and wipes his hand across his mustache with the back of his glove. He prods his horse on toward the ranch buildings, promptly followed by McGredy.

The main ranch house is a white two-story square-framed building with a wide front porch facing south. On the front steps of the planked porch sits an old rancher-type gentleman who seems intent on his wood carving in hand. He glances up at the two horseback strangers as they slowly approach and continues with his whittling.

Elkman holds up his horse and pack animal a dozen feet from the buildings and calls out.

"Hallo the house."

McGredy stays back a comfortable distance and positions behind the pack animal for protection.

"Ya got to watch these old-timers. They're just as likely to shoot as call ya in."

"We didn't come looking fer trouble and don't expect it."

Elkman throws a cautionary glance over his shoulder at the gambler and waits for a gesture to approach.

The elderly man sneaks a glimpse toward the new arrivals on horseback and waves them in while continuing his work. Elkman rides up to the front porch and stops in front of the stairs. He loops his lead rope several times around his saddle horn and leans forward.

"Howdy, sir. Lookin' fer Mister Henry Martin."

The older man looks up, squinting in the midday sun and nods. McGredy eases up next to Elkman and looks toward the front door.

"Hell of a spread . . . the feller that run this place around?"

Still intent on his wood sculpting, the man murmurs low, almost inaudible, his voice directed down toward his tall boots dangling over the steps. "Yaugh . . . ain't get many folks come a visitin' 'cept the cav'lry for remounts."

The two strain to listen as the old man appears to be finishing up a small detail on his project. Elkman waits a moment before responding to the distracted man.

"We talked with some folks at the town yonder and they said to find Henry Martin's place."

"Well, you can stop yer lookin'. Who are ya and what do you want with 'em?"

As if he just finished a masterpiece, the man raises his carving to his face and blows on it gently. Satisfied, he sets the piece of wood aside and folds the knife into his vest pocket. He rises to his feet, stretches his back, and stands on the second step, coming near eye level with the riders.

"I'm Henry Martin. Ye have some business with me?" From the leanness in his face, the rancher looks to be a man who has worked hard all his life. Wisps of grey hair curl from under his sweat-stained hat and a hard worn vest hangs on his old sturdy shoulders. He holds his callous-curled fingers before him and rubs them slowly together to work out the stiffness.

Elkman pushes up the front brim of his hat a bit and smooths his lip whiskers from his mouth.

"It was mentioned your name in a settlement not far from here about some horse work."

Henry looks the two over carefully.

"You a bronc-stomper? I know he ain't."

The comment draws McGredy's attention from the surrounding view and Elkman speaks up before the gambler can respond.

"I've worked with most animals and ain't afraid of puttin' in my time with the rougher tasks."

"Ain't no jobs available 'round here this time of season and won't be run 'em out to the high country till early summer."

Elkman nods agreeably and looks past his shoulder at the dozens of horses gazing in the valley.

"Well, sir. We might be some late, but we heard you was looking for some fellers to git horses up to another ranch in the northern territory."

"My brother's place in Montana, huh? Hell, I'd 'bout given up on that whole idea . . ."

Elkman puts his hand to his hat and readjusts it.

"If'n yer still interested, I'm Tomas H. Elkman and this here in his town clothes is Jefferson McGredy."

Henry runs his rough hard-working hands down the front of his vest and fingers the lump in his pocket where his knife sits.

"Could I trust ya to git the job done 'nd not git killt or run off with my stock?"

McGredy leans forward and spits to the side.

"You could wager on it."

Elkman sits attentive in the high cantle seat and rests both hands on the saddle horn.

"You have my word we'll do the tasks need'd doing and give you an honest job of work."

McGredy eyes Elkman sidelong and reluctantly nods in agreement. The old rancher adjusts his hat and grins as he sits back down on the porch steps.

"Hmm, somethin' to think about."

He slips a finger in his vest pocket and fishes out his carving knife again. Unfolding the small blade from the stag handle grip, he picks up his piece of wood to resume whittling.

"Why don't you two unsaddle and settle in your mounts. Git washed up in the bunkhouse. Midday grub'll be ready soon and we'll talk about it after."

Elkman puts a finger to the brim of his hat in salute and reins his horse toward the barn.

"Thank ye, sir."

McGredy watches curiously as the old man puts all his attention back to his carving project. The gambler, who is accustomed to livelier sorts of entertainment, snorts amused then steers his horse away, following Elkman to the barn.

The formal dining room of the ranch house with its ornate woodwork and papered walls looks as if it was designed for special dinners. The roughshod ways of the ranch and easy country use have turned it to more of a comfortable gathering and eating spot adjacent to the kitchen. Henry sits at the head of the table with Elkman and McGredy to each side. They watch as Henry Martin's youthful, but grown daughter clears the dishes from the meal.

Elkman gives a courteous nod toward Amy Martin as she takes away his empty plate.

"Thank you again for the meal, ma'am."

McGredy winks toward Elkman and pushes back against his creaking chair while rubbing his vested stomach.

"Yes, ma'am . . . had to skip breakfast."

After his dish setting is cleared, Henry Martin scoots his chair a bit and reaches to a side table for his pipe and smoking tobacco. He loads the clay pipe and peers up at the two men seated at his table. Through bushy eyebrows he looks to them questioningly.

"So . . . you two serious 'bout heading up north?"

McGredy puts his elbows to the table and combs his fingers through his whiskers to wipe food remnants from his beard.

"You bet we are. Been wanting to git back up that way since I left and trailin' some horseflesh for wages seems straightforward 'nough."

Henry finishes packing the pipe and lights it. He takes a few puffs and looks from McGredy to Elkman.

"Some of it's through hostile territory. Did the feller who told you happen to mention the other outfits I've sent that aways?"

Elkman wipes an errant lock of hair from his uncovered forehead and glances at his hat perched on the seat of the next chair.

"Just that you haven't had much luck with it."

Henry blows a puff of smoke and leans his chair back.

"Hell, that's one way to put it. I've lost near thirty horses and at least three good hands."

His hand stuck in his mouth, McGredy picks his teeth with his fingernail and speaks.

"Indians?"

"On the first run t'was Injuns. Who knows, could of put the fear in 'em and caused the second. Heard some of my horses were sold over in Kansas . . . hard to tell."

Elkman sits listening in the creaky ladder-back chair with his hands across his lap. He fingers the edge of the table and looks to Henry puffing on the pipe.

"Well, they're yer horses. The decision is yourn."

Henry blows out a cloud of smoke and nods. "The risk is on yer hide." He takes a short drag from his pipe. "You both willing to chance the probable run-in with Indians 'nd possible rustlers who'd just as soon kill you as look at ya?"

Folding his hands on the table, McGredy nods in agreement.

"I've covered most of the territory while scouting for the Army. Long as we stay clear of a few problem areas, I figure on less risk of run-ins with Indians."

"Maybe so."

Henry's young daughter Amy returns to the dining room and stands next to her father. "Anything else, Father?"

"No, Amy darlin', that'll do."

Amy glances around the table and gives a slight curtsy.

"I'll be seeing you gentlemen this evenin' I presume."

Elkman rises from his chair with respect. "Yes, ma'am."

McGredy half stands and bows. "It would be an honor to share your company again."

Henry smokes his pipe and observes the two prime bachelors watching his attractive young daughter's exit. He glances over his shoulder at her in the kitchen, then turns back and waits for the two to settle back in their seats.

"Well. If'n you're going to head that aways and can handle the risks, I'll send another bunch up with ya."

Elkman smiles agreeably and glances toward McGredy, who steals peeks toward the kitchen. The cowboy turns his attention back to the old rancher and rests a hand on the table.

"How many were you thinking?"

Henry rubs his chin and takes the pipe from his teeth.

"Like to get 'bout fifteen to twenty head up there. It's a long ways. I kin send one or two of my boys up there with you."

McGredy leans both elbows on the table and nods his approval. Elkman thinks a long moment and contemplates McGredy's capacity for work before responding.

"Believe one would be jest fine, that being if'n your man knows what he's doing and don't mind coming home alone when the job is done."

"You don't have to worry about 'em knowing their business. I'll send along Kent, my youngest boy with ya."

McGredy gives an uneasy cough and squirms a bit in his chair, uncomfortable. He speaks up with palpable concern.

"We can avoid the Injuns, but it's still some dangerous territory. We won't have any opportunity for teachin' or takin' care of young'uns."

Henry scoots his chair back and stands. He holds his smoking pipe cradled against his thumb as he brushes the loose tobacco and ash from his vest.

"He'll handle himself with the best of 'em. He's been wanting to git up there to look in on his uncle for quite some time."

Elkman stands and lifts his hat from the seat next to him. He holds it in hand and nods toward Henry. "Sounds like a fair arrangement. When can we have a look at them animals?"

McGredy keeps his seat and looks sour. Henry glimpses at him with a hint of a smile and moves to the doorway of the dining room. He looks back as he steps out to the porch.

"I'll let you two discuss awhile and meet you at the barn."

Elkman watches out the glass-paned door as Henry ambles down the porch steps and crosses the yard to the out-buildings. He turns to McGredy who still sits, shaking his head cynically. McGredy glances around the room, stands, and puts his hands to the table.

"I feel it. Taking his damn kid along ain't going to be nothing but trouble."

"Mister Henry Martin there said he's a good hand."

"I don't want to do no nurse-maidin' fer his youngest offspring 'less it's for that daughter of his."

"Afraid you might have to do some work?"

"It's damn sure lookin' that way."

Elkman puts on his hat and looks out to the corrals. On the far side of the barn he notices Henry's daughter Amy saddling a small buckskin gelding for an afternoon ride. A sudden surge of warmth comes over him and he looks away, embarrassed. McGredy notices the lingering stare toward the corrals and raps his knuckles on the wood table.

"See something you like?"

"Jest admirin' the setting."

"Still want to head north?"

Elkman looks to McGredy as he smirks knowingly at him.

"You still up for an honest job of work?"

Chapter 16

Leaving the ranch buildings in the background, Henry Martin leads the group as they travel horseback toward the wide, open pastures tucked between tree scattered hills. The experienced rancher rides alongside Elkman and McGredy and points out various features of the range's landscape. Approaching the herd, they converse and study the breeding stock as they ride amongst the grazing sea of four-legged animals.

Henry points out several horses while Elkman nods with approval and McGredy occasionally glances back toward the main house. The old rancher and Elkman share a common language of animal speak while enjoying the other's company. McGredy's eyes glaze over from talk of work and he lets his mind wander in daydreams of female conversation, the evening meal, or just sitting in the shade.

A rider lopes out into the valley and Henry directs his attention toward him. He repositions his horse and waits to identify the rider before speaking.

"Be right back, boys."

Putting heels to hide, Henry trots his horse to the messenger and converses awhile. Elkman glances toward McGredy as he moves up next to him. He grins at the aloof gambler who appears uninterested and out of his element.

"Enjoying yerself?"

"Damned bored out'a my skull if you ain't noticed."

"Mister Martin sure knows his horseflesh and has a knack for makin' some fine animals."

McGredy stretches his back in the saddle and shakes his head.

"I know as much about horses as I'll e'er need to."

He motions to his horse sarcastically.

"This here is the head, that's the tail, the saddle goes here, and my rule is to keep the horse between me 'nd the ground."

Elkman smiles and scratches his chin.

"Ye seem to have the basics."

"If that old man keeps us out here another hour tellin' us which horse came from which, I'll just fall asleep and tumble down from here."

"And break your rudimentary horse rule?"

McGredy looks sidelong at Elkman and grunts.

"You know . . . half the time I don't even think you listen to what I'm saying, then you go 'nd throw a zinger at me."

He wags his finger at Elkman.

"I'm gonna have to watch you, T. H., for you just might have some card-partner potential yet."

"Don't get yer hopes up."

"I jest play the odds."

They observe as the horseback messenger lopes back toward the barn and Henry waves them over. Elkman indicates to the distant rancher and faintly smiles under his lip whiskers toward McGredy.

"I kinder enjoy hearing someone speak who knows what they're talking about for a change."

"Since when do you enjoy good conversation?"

"It's more education than conversation."

"I'll keep my talk of breeding for the bordellos."

"We all have our areas of experience."

Elkman gives a prod to his mount and McGredy follows at a lope with his head tilted far-back and exaggerates a snoring sound.

The three horseback men ride in from the pastures. For an aged man, Henry sits tallest in the saddle, followed by Elkman, then McGredy, who sits loose and indifferent. They all ease to a trot as they near the barn. A young man steps out from the shade of the building and watches as they approach.

Dressed in well-used chaps and a hard worn, sweat-stained hat, Kent Martin looks the old-hand with exception to his boyish face and lack of chin stubble. He watches the men quietly as his father sidesteps his horse near to him.

"Hello Kent, my boy . . . wondered if you were going to be in from the range tonight."

Kent studies the unfamiliar riders then looks up at his father.

"I brought in a few that drifted on the west valley. Other than that, everything is looking dandy."

"Fellas, this here is my youngest boy, Kent Martin."

Elkman touches the brim of his hat and glances toward McGredy who studies the young cowboy. Henry scratches his belly beneath his vest as he continues the introduction.

"Kent, this here is Tomas H. Elkman and Mister Jefferson McGredy. They're going to trail them horses up to yer Uncle James in the north country for us."

Elkman moves his horse forward and extends his hand down to the young man. Kent shakes his outstretched offer and nods toward McGredy.

"How many you planning on sending, this time?"

Under the young man's probing eye, Elkman sits confident as the old rancher answers. "Figured 'bout fifteen."

Kent pulls off his stained leather glove and smacks it on the leg of his chaps. He looks up to McGredy, then Elkman.

"He tell you what happened to the others we sent?"

Elkman leans down on the saddle horn. "He did."

Kent and Elkman size each other up a long moment until the young man looks back to his father.

"It's a sizable risk."

"Was wondering if'n you might go along as a third hand?"

Kent glances over at McGredy and sniffs.

"Do these fellers know horses or am I to do all the work?"

Elkman gives an amused smile and McGredy shifts in the saddle, his temper rising. Henry looks back to the house and nods absentmindedly. "I think they're capable."

McGredy nudges his horse a few steps closer and looks down at Kent. "Boy, you're gonna have to know a lot more than jest horses to get through that country up there."

"I know all about what's up there!"

"You ever forked a saddle north of Denver?"

"No, but I know more about it than you, most likely."

McGredy glares at Kent and lowers his voice to a murmur.

"The hell you do . . . yer just a young wet 'hind the ears pup. I've been scoutin' Injuns since you were still on the teet."

Although McGredy speaks low, Elkman and Mr. Martin hear the talk plain and watch, slightly amused. Kent puffs up and stares angrily at McGredy.

"Step down from there and call me pup!"

Elkman rests his hand on the saddle horn and watches while Henry climbs down from his mount and tosses his reins over the hitching rail. The old rancher scratches the side of his boot on the post and glances toward his son.

"Mind yer manners, Kent. We ain't looking for a fight. If'n you don't want to go speak now."

Kent stares at McGredy who smiles down at him smugly. The boy jerks the brim of his hat down near his eyes and nods.

"When do we leave?"

Henry holds an arm across his body and leans back on the creaky barn door. He eyes the group of men before him awhile and sighs, satisfied.

"I figure to round up a few on the east pasture and the rest from the south. I made a list."

Henry removes a small tally book and pencil from his vest pocket and tears off the top page.

"Pull one of the boys to help you on the morrow and ye can be on yer way the day after."

Kent takes the paper from his father and tucks it in the leather flap pocket on his chaps. He glances up at Elkman, then over at McGredy, and steps away from the barn entrance. He calls over his shoulder as he rounds the corner. "Meet ya both in the east pasture come mornin' . . . 'nd be ready to work."

Elkman glances at McGredy and they exchange an entertained look. Not one to dawdle, Elkman nudges his horse forward and lowers his head under the barn door frame, riding his animal back toward the stalls. Henry follows after and McGredy remains.

The gambler pats the dust off his clothing and looks out, assessing the lush ranch surroundings and the trail leading away to the inviting escape of the distant hills.

Chapter 17

The early morning sky is still a dark purplish hue before the sun crests the horizon. A single oil lantern illuminates the inside of the horse barn as Elkman and McGredy saddle their horses. McGredy rubs the sleep from his eyes as he leans on the animal's rib cage then tightens his cinch.

"Gol-damn Tomas. This is ridiculous, going out to round up horses before the sun comes up. Don't them four-legged critters need sleep too?"

He rests on the saddle skirting and looks over at Elkman.

"'Fore I met you . . . this was about the time I would call it quits at the gamin' tables."

Elkman coils his braided rawhide rope and works out a kink in the loop. He glances over to McGredy who looks near asleep while standing against his horse.

"If'n we're gonna set that kid straight 'nd not have problems with 'em later, we're gonna have to work on ranch time. When we're on the trail we can adjust the schedule accordingly."

Elkman drapes his riata over the slick fork horn of his saddle and gives his horse a gentle pat.

"No one is holdin' a gun to yer head to work."

"That'd be something."

McGredy watches Elkman swing up to the saddle. He shakes the sleep from his head then puts his left foot in the stirrup. With a groan, McGredy hoists himself topside and squints tired eyes toward Elkman.

"Yeah, I get it . . . I can jest go my own way."

Elkman grins as he trots his horse out of the barn into the early light of morning. McGredy pulls his coat tight around his neck and shakes off the predawn chill.

"Damn cowboys are a mite more enjoyable to take money from than earn it with."

McGredy exits the barn and lopes after Elkman into the glowing light of the not yet risen sun over the quiet valley.

A cool haze of fog-like mist rises from the damp grasses of the adjoining pastures. The blaze-orange sun pokes over the hills to the east and silhouettes two cowboys horseback, standing and waiting. McGredy moves his horse up next to Elkman and they slow to a walking approach. McGredy shakes his head, annoyed, and spits with contempt for the early risers.

"I'll be damned . . ."

"Feels he's got some provin' to do."

"That kid must'a damn near slept out here."

Elkman and McGredy ride up at a steady trot while Kent gives the cowboy alongside a nudge to wake him. Elkman touches his gloved hand to the brim of his hat and nods.

"Morning, Kent."

Kent acknowledges the nod while he shuffles his rope and feigns impatience to work. McGredy grumbles. "Sleep much?"

Kent glances between McGredy and Elkman then speaks to the cowboy sitting alongside.

"C'mon, let's get to work."

Elkman exchanges a glance with McGredy and they both look at the young man so eager to prove his authority. The sleepy gambler scratches his beard and pushes back in the saddle to lounge.

"I thought we'd visit awhile and enjoy the sunrise."

"The work don't get done sittin' around."

"Life don't get enjoyed chasing away the mornin'."

The cowboy beside Kent nods, looking to the early light of the sun coming over the mountains. Kent gives the cowhand a slap across the arm with the back of his hand and whines. "Ya want me to git ya a cup of coffee too?"

In the early light of day, the trail partners look to each other, amused. Elkman smiles and wipes his fingers across his mustache.

"Lead the way, sir."

Kent stifles his irritation and gives his mount a jab of his spurred boot-heels. He tears off across the pasture toward the slumbering horse herd with rope in hand. McGredy squints questioningly to the other sleepy-eyed cowboy.

"How long you been out here?"

The cowboy rubs the sleep from his face and eases his horse in the direction of Kent.

"Probably 'bout an hour . . . "

The cowboy rides away and McGredy slaps his hat on his leg, shaking his head, perturbed.

"Once we're on the trail away from this damned ranch, we'd better cure 'em of these bad habits quick."

Elkman smiles and gives his horse a tap.

"Yup."

The morning shines bright down on the lush green valley as the four riders gather horses for the trail north. Each green-broke horse is roped, inspected, and tied to a hitch line. With all the chasing and wrangling of horseflesh involved, McGredy is often sitting to the side observing instead of working.

As the last horse is gathered and put with the others, Kent looks up at the midday sun and coils his rope.

"Not a bad morning's work, hope you fellas don't waste 'em on the trail. The man who rides the morning has a job for another day."

Elkman rides over as he loops his rope.

"Yer paw say that?"

"He does."

McGredy rides near and sniffs snidely.

"We'll have you to watch o'er us."

Kent glances over his shoulder at McGredy then unties a string of five horses. He holds the lead rope and trails the stock out in a nice lineup behind him.

"All set to head back?"

He gives the rope a tug and pulls inline one of the skittish mares.

"We'll corral them in the north lot, behind the barn."

Several of the animals bite at each other and balk until Kent guides them in a wide marching circle. He holds the lead rope behind him taut, and with the string of five horses in tow, trots back toward the barn. The other cowboy yanks the ground-tie loose for another string of five animals and follows.

Elkman pulls a glove off and wipes the sweat from his forehead as McGredy eases his horse nearer. They both watch as the two sets of horses crest the rise in the noontime sun. McGredy clicks his teeth and scratches his whiskers.

"That kid is going to be a pain."

"I'm starting on the same opinion."

"No wonder they want to send him north."

Elkman slides his hand back in his glove and rides over to the remaining picketed horse string. He tugs the long grass the lead rope is tied to and unties the knot at the end. Tossing several long stalks of pasture aside, Elkman shrugs.

"The old man probably taught him to be like that."

McGredy follows Elkman along and raises his chin annoyed.

"Suppose it's too late to ditch the asshead?"

The two sit their horses alongside another, faced in opposite directions and Elkman grins with a nod.

"Yaugh, suppose it is."

Elkman leans over and wraps the last horse string lead rope around McGredy's saddle horn.

"Go on 'nd run 'em in. I'm gonna have a look around."

McGredy studies Elkman a bit, curious of his intentions. "Where you goin'?"

"Jest to survey the size of the spread."

The reluctant gambler takes the rope in hand and looks around.

"It all probably looks like this."

"Could be."

Giving a sidelong glance, McGredy hints a smile. "Don't go runnin' off on me."

"Why would I go 'nd leave such a hard workin' partner such as yerself?"

"Partner now, huh? I knowed I'd grow on ya."

With a tug of the lead rope, McGredy trails the string of horses toward the path followed by the others back to the barn.

Elkman watches the string of horse stock disappear over the ridge and looks around at the lingering animals as they graze the valley and the tree-covered hills all around. He inhales the peaceful serenity of life in the present and turns his mount away from the trodden path. Trotting to an easy lope, Elkman cuts through the lulling herd and moves out toward the surrounding landscapes.

Chapter 18

The hillside is quiet and still as Elkman maneuvers his horse at a walk through the trees and comes over the top to another valley narrower than the last. He eases his horse down the grade and sits in the saddle observing from the edge of the tree-line. Across the open space, he spies a saddled horse idly grazing and someone sitting on the ground nearby. He casts an eye over the area to familiarize himself with the surroundings. Holding back a moment to listen for any sound of distress, Elkman prods his horse on and rides across the valley.

Upon nearing the empty-saddled horse, Elkman recognizes Henry Martin's daughter Amy sitting in the long grass with a book in her lap. He slows his loping gait as she looks up and he stops a short distance away.

"Howdy, ma'am."

"Hello there, Mister Elkman."

"Reading?"

The attractive girl closes her book and pulls back a lock of hair that had fallen across her face.

"I was until you bravely rescued me from the boredom of this tome, Mister Elkman."

Elkman shifts his hat on his head, uncomfortable in her attentions.

"Ye can jest call me Tomas."

"Or Tom . . . perhaps?"

"I prefer Tomas."

"Then you can call me Amy."

"Yes, ma'am."

There is a silent pause as Amy looks up at the horseback cowboy and studies him. She absentmindedly rubs her hand across the cover of her book and smiles.

"You finished playing with those horses?"

An awkward feeling consumes Elkman and he starts to regret the interaction. He takes up his reins and looks over his shoulder.

"Figured I'd ride around a bit. Beautiful country."

"Yes, it is. Have you seen enough of it yet?"

"Naw . . . I ne'er get my fill of the out o' doors. I could ride here all day."

A chill of excitement mixed with dread surges through Elkman as he watches Amy stand, brush her skirt off, and go to her horse. She tucks the leather bound book in her saddlebag, buckles it closed, and turns to the horseback cowboy.

"Sounds good to me."

A bit surprised at her forwardness, Elkman removes his hat and sweeps back his sweat-curled hair.

"Uh . . . Miss Martin. I don't know if it would be proper?"

Amy tightens her cinch and swings up into the saddle. She adjusts her skirting and takes up the reins to her horse.

"Will you be buttonholing me for ransom, Tomas?"

"No, ma'am . . . can't say I know what that is?"

"Will you be accosting me?"

"No, ma'am."

"Then there is nothing improper about it."

Elkman wipes his fingers around the damp leather sweatband inside his hat and places it back on his head.

"I jest mean . . . a young lady such as yerself shouldn't be out here riding alone."

"Such as myself . . . what does that mean?"

"Uh, well . . . I mean unaccompanied."

"Well, then you'll have to accompany me."

Elkman looks around uncertain as Amy nudges her mount and rides away. She looks over her shoulder and waves him on.

"Come along, Tomas!"

With another quick glance around, Elkman jabs his spurs to his horse and readily follows after Amy.

In the wide expanse of nature, Elkman and Amy ride alongside one another, each enjoying the quiet solitude all around. Elkman relaxes into the saddle and relishes the peaceful moment of companionship. The pair travels through sparse trees and grazed meadows until Amy steals a glance over at Elkman and finally breaks the lingering silence.

"Where are you from, Tomas H. Elkman?"

He thinks a moment and replies casual. "Nowhere in particular."

Amy grins and shakes her long hair away from her shoulder. "You have to be from somewhere."

Elkman nods and turns to look at her.

"I grew up a ways east of here."

"That's still not a place."

"Where I grew up wasn't much of a place either."

"Everyone comes from somewhere."

The horses walk along unhurried and Elkman stares ahead.

"I'd rather be going somewhere than lookin' back."

"If this is going to work . . . our conversation I mean. You'll have to learn to talk more in detail."

Amy smiles at him and he turns to catch a glimpse, then looks ahead. Uncomfortable in her gaze, he pulls his hat down a bit.

"Well, where are you from?"

"Here . . . but I was schooled out east awhile. I lived with my Mother mostly."

"Where's she at?"

"She is enjoying the perks of city life. My father loves her, but she doesn't love the ranch."

"What'd ya come back for?"

"A better life."

Elkman smiles and looks over at her, amused.

"You funnin' me? Most womenfolk figure it the other way 'round. It's a random pleasure to talk with a gal who ain't longin' for flower paper'd walls and fancy dish parties."

Amy glances over with a sultry look.

"Let's just say I tended to overindulge on the city life. My mother wanted me there to make a lady of me. It didn't quite have that effect."

"She send you back?"

"No. I decided I didn't want to become that person. I returned here to live a more fulfilling life where the things that are important really matter. After a time in the city, you just kind of lose sight of yourself if you're not careful."

Elkman nods and stares away into the distance.

"That can happen anywhere, I suppose."

They ride along silently again, each looking out to the beauty of nature around them. A reprieve from conversation, Elkman takes in a breath, steals a glance toward the fine-looking girl riding alongside him, and smiles, genuinely relieved. His horse reaches out and nuzzles the neck of the nearby filly and he feels a similar longing. Amy turns to Elkman and smiles sweetly.

"Where do you call home?"

Elkman lifts his hat by the crown, points to the opening inside and smiles a humorous grin.

"Here."

The amused look of the striking female puts Elkman ill at ease and he replaces his head covering. She beams at him and runs her hand through the hair at the nape of her neck.

"Do you move around a lot?"

"Some."

"Why?"

"There's a lot to see."

Elkman timidly adjust his hat and Amy grins playfully.

"You're going to wear out that poor old hat of yours."

As almost by reflex, Elkman touches his hat again.

"Jest things I don't usually talk about."

"Why?"

"Gosh, you talk more'n McGredy does."

"Has he been your friend awhile?"

"Not long."

"How did you meet?"

"I'd rather not talk 'bout it."

Amy lean over her horse's neck and combs the mane with her long slender fingers. "Do you ever get tired of moving around?

"No, not much."

"Ever get lonely?"

"Now 'nd again. I think how it could be elsewheres and things don't look so bad."

"What's the alternative? Settling down in one place, chasing a life-time of work ahead of you? Being like my father and the ranch?"

Elkman shakes his head to the negative.

"No . . . like mine. I've just come to love the land in a different way."

"He was a farmer?"

"He tried."

Amy looks over at Elkman and smiles teasingly.

"Do you have a pleasure-filled, exciting life of adventure, Mister Tomas H. Elkman?"

"I have interestin' recollections. When they're in the middle of hap-penin' it's usually hard to enjoy 'em."

They continue to ride along and Amy stares at Elkman a long, atten-tive while, seeming to study his every move and being.

"You are a curious fellow. You don't seem like the others that chase horses. Or like that Jefferson McGredy you're with for that matter."

She looks down at his walnut handled pistol grip perched in his hol-ster at his side.

"Are you a pistoleer?"

Elkman smiles and shakes his head in deference to the claim.

"I'm no Wild Bill."

"What are you looking to find, moving around all the time?"

"I just don't want to ever feel stuck."

She gives a flirtatious laugh and smile.

"Unless it's the right place, or the right time perhaps?"

Elkman grins and rubs his finger across his mustache.

"I suppose."

"Do you want children?"

"If I had me a wife first."

A glint or mischievousness flashes in Amy's eyes.

"Will that ever happen?"

"With the right gal, I could settle on a dozen little 'uns."

Amy takes a deep breath and smooths her form-fitting blouse over her abdomen. She smiles at Elkman and shakes her head gently.

"I shouldn't probably be seen riding alone with a ruffian like yourself. My mother has already put the caution to Pappy. It was nice riding and talking with you, Tomas."

Elkman nods and put his fingertips to the brim of his hat.

"You're a breath of fresh air, Miss Amy."

Amy gives her horse a kick and lopes away. She looks over her shoulder and calls out sweetly.

"Hope you know that time and place someday when you come across it."

Elkman half-heartedly holds back on the reins to keep his eager mount from following. He sits tall in the saddle and watches the shapely form of the young woman ride across the meadow toward her settled life and the ranch setting in the distance.

Chapter 19

In the black hours before daybreak, the door opens to the bunk house and a dark shadow approaches with a dimmed oil lantern. The figure walks to Elkman's bunk, pauses briefly then moves past. The dark form stands at the next low-sunk bunk and turns the lamp wick brighter directly over McGredy's sleeping body. The sounds of slumber continue steadily and the lantern is directed over the snoring man's head. With the light held high, the young, fresh face of Kent is illuminated.

"Wake up, boys. Time to git going."

McGredy wriggles his mouth and chin whiskers but lies still with his eyes remaining closed. A stern countenance crosses his face as his eyelids twitch from the bright light.

"If'n you don't git that lamp out of my face and this shack in two 'nd a half seconds, I'm gonna wallop you and send you cryin' to yer Pa."

Kent stands dismayed and unsure what to do.

"One . . ."

His slumber disturbed, Elkman rolls over and opens an eye.

"Don't push it kid."

McGredy growls.

"Two . . ."

Kent turns toward Elkman who still appears to be sleeping, then grudgingly backs out the door with the lamp. The rope-supported bed creaks with strain as McGredy flops over with a grunt and grumbles.

"I swear . . . that kid is gonna git a whaling 'fore we even leave this place."

Elkman pulls up his blanket and fades back into slumber.

"He'll come 'round."

The call of a rooster rattles through the stillness as Elkman and McGredy step out from the bunkhouse into the chilled early light of day. With stowed blanket-rolls tucked under arms, they walk the short distance to the horse barn. Inside the tall, open doors, they walk down the center breezeway. A horse stands tied and waiting to be saddled as Kent lies nearby, asleep on a pile of straw. The boy clutches his rope and a new six-shooter pistol belt hangs around his hips over his leather chaps.

Elkman shakes his head as he walks past and McGredy stands over the young cowboy and snorts.

"What an asshead. . . . I'm half tempted to put my boot to 'em jest to teach him a lesson."

Elkman looks back on the boy's peaceful slumber.

"Let 'em be. . . . For some, the hard way's the only way to learn."

"Hell, this kid has been discourteous and a pain in my backside from the start."

Elkman pulls his lead rope from a peg and enters his animal's stall.

"Do what you want to do."

The morning smell of the barn hangs in the air as McGredy stands over the sleeping boy. He stares down at Kent cozily asleep and contemplates waking him. After a moment, he leans down and unbuckles Kent's gun-belt and refastens it a few notches looser. He then looks to the kid's spurs dangling off his boot heels and glances over while Elkman leads his mount from the stall.

"Should I lash his spurs together?"

"It won't endear you to him much."

"I ain't trying to win no popularity contest."

"It's a long ways to Montana."

McGredy nods and thinks a minute. He struts past Elkman to his own horse's stall and whispers loudly.

"I guess I'll need that hard workin' kid to make up for my own tendency to do less."

"You will at that."

Elkman ties off his horse and looks over to the young cowboy calmly sleeping despite the stirring sounds from the stable animals.

Elkman and McGredy lead their saddled horses through the barn as Henry Martin approaches from the main house. Walking past the still sleeping boy, Elkman gives him a nudge with his boot.

"Best look alive . . ."

The teenager wakes just as his father enters the barn. Instantly alert and jumping to his feet, Kent's loose gun-belt tumbles around his ankles. Henry stares at his young son questioningly as Kent pulls up the cartridge belt and cinches it tighter. The old man looks to Elkman and McGredy with their already saddled mounts.

"Morning boys. You're all up early."

McGredy glances over at Kent and smirks.

"Yaugh, figured we'd git an early start. They say, the man who rides the morning has work for another day."

Henry smiles knowingly and frowns when he looks to Kent.

"Where's your horse, boy?"

Kent stammers as he rubs the sleep from his eyes.

"I was just about to get her ready, sir."

Shaking his head displeased, Henry looks to Elkman apologetically.

"He's typically the first one up."

The old rancher steps toward his son.

"I'm sending you along to help these fellers, not to hold them back. If'n you're not up to it, let me know now."

McGredy steps away and mumbles under his breath.

"It'll take more'n just new gun-leather."

The young boy looks to Elkman who nods reassuringly. He looks to his father and stands straight.

"I'm up to it, sir."

Kent stands uncomfortably under his father's scrutinizing eye and steals a glance toward McGredy, who pretends to ignore him. The father pats the boy on the shoulder and gives him a shove.

"Well, go git your horse then."

Kent's spurs jingle as he jogs through the barn and quickly goes to his horse. McGredy turns away smiling and kindly rubs on the ear of his mount. The old rancher watches a moment, then turns to face the two men and shakes his head rueful.

"Sorry 'bout that. He's usually a pretty hard worker."

Elkman twirls the end of his reins and nods.

"Not a problem, he'll be alright on the trail."

"I'm sure he will be. If'n he ain't you just turn 'em on his tail and send him home."

Henry watches Kent throw his saddle and cinch up. He shakes his head disappointedly again and looks out the wide doors to the rising sun. Motioning for Elkman and McGredy to follow, he walks to exit the barn.

"Come along boys . . . let's get them horses together so you can be on yer way."

McGredy grins at Elkman and, with a sweeping bow, ushers him after the old man.

"After you, sir."

"You loosen that kid's holster belt?"

McGredy looks to Elkman agape with an angelic innocence. "Why would I do such a thing?"

"Suppose he jest lost a few inches during his siesta."

Elkman frowns, amused, looks back at Kent hustling his gear together, and follows the rancher outside.

In the fence corral at the south side of the ranch buildings, the horses are assembled in three strings of animals. A short length of rope looped around their necks and tied to a lead line, the breeding stock occasionally reaches out to nip and bite at the nearest mare.

McGredy waits and watches horseback inside the wood rail fence as Elkman rides circles while inspecting the animals. The young boy with something to prove takes the first string and trots them over to his father at the gate. Henry reaches out and places a paternal hold on Kent's leg.

"Take care, boy. Do all you can to git them horses up to your uncle, but don't be foolish. Remember, they're just animals. They can be replaced."

"Yes, sir."

The rancher gives the boy's leg a pat and swipes a callused finger past a tear-glazed eye. As Kent rides out of the corral, Henry runs his hand over each animal as it passes. He mumbles to himself about the horses' configuration and nods quietly.

McGredy waits on horseback near the fence observing the work going on, and the rancher looks up at him.

"It was good to meet you, Mister McGredy. You take care of my boy there and he'll work hard for ya."

"We'll git 'em north."

Henry nods and walks over to Elkman as he unties the second string of animals. He steps around the line of horses and reaches into his vest to pull out a folded letter.

"Give that letter to my brother James when you git north and he'll compensate you as agreed. There is also a document of transfer for the stock."

Elkman pulls off one of his gloves and takes the letter. He tucks it in his shirt pocket inside his vest and extends his hand down to the waiting rancher.

"Thank you for your trust, sir. We'll do our best for ya and keep watch o'er that kin of yourn."

Henry brushes his cheek as he peers out from under the brim of his hat into the rising sun and rakes his fingernails down through his gray stubble whiskers.

"I know you will. Hopefully our paths will cross again. If'n you have a mind to head back with Kent, there'll be a job for ye here. Good luck to ya, wherever you might end up."

Elkman watches the old man and feels the faint longing for a home and something to build upon. He glances to the house and pats his breast pocket with the sale letter.

"We'll have the horses up there after a few weeks if all goes fine 'nd well. We'll send news when we can."

Henry gives a nod and steps back from Elkman's path. He takes up the third string of animals and hands it off to McGredy. The old rancher holds the gate open and Elkman leads out of the corral, followed by the last grouping. With the posture of a seasoned cowboy, Henry climbs and swings a leg over the wood fence rail while still holding the gate and waves them off.

"Git on out of here! Enjoy the journey boys, hee-jaww!"

Raising a hand in salute from the brim of his Stetson, Elkman rides past the porch of the house and momentarily pauses as McGredy trots by.

"Ye forget somethin'?"

Elkman shakes his head and glances to his reflection in the wavy glass window panes of the dining room. He gives the lead rope a tug and lopes after McGredy.

They join Kent at the end of the fence row and ride for the hills to the north. Henry watches as the three cowboys lead the capering line of fresh horses across the valley and over the horizon. He lets the gate slip from his hold and it slowly swings closed on the hinge with a creak and a bang.

The solitary rancher looks back at the main house, watches a curtain flutter upstairs, and gives a sniff. Unhooking his leg from the rail, the old cowboy drops to the ground and ambles to the barn. The activity of the morning is continued by the regular hands rousing from breakfast in the bunkhouse and preparing for the day's work.

The three horsemen trail the herd of horses north several days through picturesque sceneries of rock, trees, and sky. Occasionally to the far west, the snow-capped peaks of the Rockies can be seen on the skyline. In the lower elevations, the steady clop of hooves raises a haze of dust that clings close while the overhead sun bakes down on them as they pass across broad landscapes.

Elkman pulls his horse to a halt and scans the lesser range of mountains before them in the north. He ponders awhile as Kent and McGredy ride up alongside him. In the moment of pause, the trailing horse stock take advantage and lower their heads to graze the tall dry grass left standing from the previous fall. Elkman puts a leg over the pommel of his saddle and pats the trail dust from his thigh and knee.

"We'll set up camp here for the night."

McGredy looks to the rough terrain ahead leading into the mountains and nods in agreement. He stretches his back and rubs the inner side of his leg.

"I ain't ridden so much since I worked for US Grant."

Kent eases up next to Elkman and looks to the path ahead.

"Set up camp here already? We still have about an hour of daylight yet."

Pushing his hat back on his forehead a bit, Elkman looks at Kent and leans forward in his posture.

"In an hour we'll be right up in those hills and then where do you suppose we set up camp and keep the stock?"

Kent spins his mount with an agitated seat in the saddle and tosses the lead rope for his stock string to keep from getting tangled. The horses move away, dropping their heads to eat, and step nearer the other groupings. Kent sits his horse rigid and jerks him to a standstill.

"We could still git a bit farther."

McGredy laughs as he dismounts.

"Why?"

"Cause it's the job."

Elkman loosens his rawhide riata from the leather saddle tie and tosses it to the ground ahead of them.

"Yer gonna have to learn to live outside the ranch. You watch Jefferson and myself awhile 'nd you might learn a thing or two about life."

They look over to see McGredy digging in his nose.

"Well, not McGredy so much."

Kent spins his horse again and sets his jaw.

"I'm gonna ride out ahead and check things out."

"Suit yerself."

Elkman drops the lead rope to let the animals graze and steers his horse toward where McGredy stands.

"Jefferson, what type of native populations are we dealing with here-abouts?"

His hat removed, McGredy comes from around his horse scratching his hair and looks up to Elkman and Kent.

"Should be clear yet fer the next few days or so. Jest be sure to watch for signs of 'em. Pony tracks, campfires 'nd such."

"I know what a damn Injun sign looks like . . ."

Kent grimaces and puts spurs to hide, racing off to the north in a thunder of hooves and slapping leather. Elkman shakes his head and adjusts his hat down on his forehead. McGredy peers up at him horseback and snorts.

"That boy is jest itchin' for a fight of some kind."

"Hopefully he don't draw after you."

McGredy sniffs and walks away.

"I don't go lookin' for fight, they jest kinder find me."

"They seem to find you more'n most."

The tired gambler turns and grins.

"Most good things in life seem to find me more'n most."

Elkman turns his attention from McGredy to the young cowboy as he disappears galloping through the hills.

Chapter 20

The late afternoon sky darkens into evening as Elkman and McGredy sit around a small campfire. The short flames jump and pop, giving off little heat but ample light. The two quietly break off pieces of hard tack and chew on the sustenance. McGredy perks his head slightly and listens into the distance. He looks to Elkman with a hint of concern.

"Suppose he run into trouble?"

"Could be."

"Pace he was travelin' tis possible he tumbled that steed."

"Cain't do much if he ain't got sense enough to git back 'fore dark."

McGredy wipes crumbs from his vest and stares off into the night.

"What the hell was he lookin' for anyway?"

"Just wants to prove himself."

"He done proved himself in the wrong ways already."

The faint tread of hooves is felt through the ground and the nicker of a horse is heard approaching. Touching their guns at the ready, they both squint into the darkness.

"Haloo the camp!"

Elkman and McGredy stand with rifles in hand. Elkman pulls back the long-arm's hammer and steps away from the firelight.

"Come on then."

His horse winded and well sweated, Kent rides up and dismounts. McGredy walks toward him and looks past to his dark back-trail.

"What put the burr under yer saddle, boy?"

Elkman stands just outside the circle of firelight.

"Ya run into trouble?"

Kent drops his reins to the ground and unfastens the cinch on his saddle. He pulls his rig and blanket and tosses them near the campfire.

"No trouble . . . but we should watch for it."

McGredy stands near Kent as he spreads his blanket over his saddle to dry near the small fire.

"Indians?"

"None that I saw."

"Them's the worst kind."

Kent looks up at McGredy, scornful, then rises and walks around the big man to his horse. He leads his sweated mount to the picket line, unbridles him, and ties a hobble between the two front legs.

Still watching, but satisfied with the absence of unwanted visitors, Elkman returns to the firelight and waits for Kent.

"What did you find out there?"

"I met up with two riders."

"What type were they?"

Kent looks over at McGredy then Elkman, both standing around the small campfire. The young boy looks a touch more mature with the hue of the flames reflecting on his sweated face under the wide brim of his hat.

"Rustlin' type."

Laying down his rifle, McGredy snorts and sits back on the ground next to his saddle.

"How the hell would you know what the rustlin' type is? You ever been mixed up with anything outside yer homestead?"

Kent stands closer to the fire and glares down at McGredy.

"I know your type well enough."

McGredy jumps to his feet, standing opposite Kent with the small campfire between them.

"What're you implying, pup?"

The two stare each other down until Elkman steps up and taps McGredy on the chest with the broadside of his rifle.

"Simmer down now, the both of ya."

"I'll not be insulted by this wet 'hind-the-ears tenderfoot."

"I'm game, tinhorn!"

Kent puffs up and inches closer until Elkman swings the barrel of his rifle over and lays it across Kent's ribcage. The soft blow takes some of the wind out of Kent's posture and they both look to Elkman as he speaks, low and direct.

"The one looking to get a length of gun barrel laid across his skull can make the first move."

McGredy and Kent stare at each other another hostile minute until the larger man backs off.

"Yer not worth soiling my boots ta kick the shit out of. Someday when you weigh more'n a buck 'nd a quarter, I'll accommodate ya."

Kent stares at the hulking form of McGredy in the low light of the campfire and glances toward Elkman, who shakes his head while lowering his rifle.

"Ye should pick fights more to yer size."

Kent looks away and sits by his gear near the fire and McGredy follows suit, sitting across.

All seems quiet in the dark environs of night. Elkman stares into the blackness and listens a moment before squatting on his haunches between the two, holding his rifle at his side pointed skyward. He uncocks the hammer and looks around the camp circle.

"Now that everyone's calmed a bit, let's hear what the kid has to say."

Elkman turns to Kent and waits for him to settle in.

"What was it about these two riders that 'rose suspicion?"

With his dander still up a bit, Kent looks from Elkman to McGredy and back again.

"Don't know what it was exactly, but they seemed to keep asking about the horses and how many riders."

McGredy takes a fleeting look over his shoulder and leans in toward Kent. "Did they ask where we're headed?"

"Yep, wanted to know distance and how soon we planned to be there too."

Elkman listens patiently as he lays his rifle across his lap.

"What did you tell them?"

"I didn't hardly tell them anything."

Kent pauses and looks between them both hesitantly. McGredy grunts angrily. "How much didn't you tell them?"

"Don't know exactly. I didn't get suspicious till late in the conversation."

McGredy kicks his heels in the ground and pouts.

"Hell boy, you done set us up for an ambush."

Elkman displays a quieting palm of his hand toward McGredy.

"Hold on, Jefferson. We don't know their intentions for sure." He looks to Kent. "Ya just felt a suspicion, right?" Kent thinks quietly and looks at the fire. McGredy's temper rises and he barks in a low voice.

"What's it gonna be?"

"I'm not sure. Thinking on it, I cain't tell."

Elkman stands and steps away from the campfire, looking around into the darkness and holding his rifle cautious.

"It won't be tonight most likely. We best get some sleep and think on it on the morrow."

He looks down at Kent and the young man looks up at him sheepishly. "Get some grub, tend to yer gear, and kick out that fire." Elkman turns to McGredy. "I'll stand first watch tonight and we'll run a cold camp till we know we're clear."

McGredy nods as he lies back on his saddle and pulls his rifle near.

"Damn . . . hardly a week out and we already have rustlers sniffin' at our heels."

Kent opens his war bag and takes out a piece of jerky. He chews off a bite and kicks out the fire with his boot heel, leaving the amber glow of coals and occasional pop of flame.

Chapter 21

The coolness of morning brings an unspoken tension as the three trail hands pack up and gather the horses. Their morning tasks are troubled by the feelings of watchers upon them. Ready to depart, Elkman climbs into the saddle and scans the misty horizon. He holds the braided lead rope for his string of horses in his right hand and the split reins to his own bridle in his left.

The empty landscape all around is calm and the rough mountainous terrain ahead looms ominously, shrouded in haze. Elkman looks down at the dark walnut stock of his rifle protruding from the saddle scabbard tucked through his rawhide riata. He gives the rifle butt a tap, gauges the distance for easy reach, and seems satisfied with the state of matters. The mount paws the ground impatient and Elkman situates himself in the saddle before turning back to the others as they mount up.

"Let's git moving."

McGredy rides along next to Elkman with his string of horses in tow. He glances back at young Kent and speaks low.

"Keep a sharp eye for any sort of tracks or trail which might tell us the way they're headed."

Elkman nods and prods his mount forward. The two ride ahead toward the fog obscured mountains as Kent brings up the drag position, following attentively behind.

The trail twists along narrow, high-country animal paths at the approach to the mountain territory. Wary of the steep edge and the drop below, the three horsemen lead their string of animals carefully along. The morning hours are spent traveling upwards through the rocky terrain and they finally start their descent well after mid-day. Despite the treacherous path, each rider seems distracted, occasionally watching the trail behind and the distant valley beyond.

Rocks crunch and tumble down from the trail as the riders hug the inside wall and brush their legs and stirrups against the steep stone face. In the lead, Elkman rounds a bend and pauses, looking ahead at the partially eroded path. He raises his hand, gesturing to halt the others behind, and studies the access across.

Everyone holds in waiting as Elkman contemplates for a long minute. He looks back at his trailing animals, the lead rope connecting them all, and the other groupings of horses waiting on the narrow mountain trail. McGredy hollers from the lineup and breaks the tense silence.

"What hails? Something up there Tomas?"

Elkman swivels in the saddle and calls back.

"Trail's near washed out."

McGredy peers over at the steep drop-off and rocky boulder scree below from the edge of the mountainside cut.

"Can we git across? I don't take kindly to the thought of trying to turn these critters on this goat trail."

Elkman studies the slender, broken out path ahead and considers their options.

"We kin make it, but if one of these animals missteps I don't want to lose the whole bunch."

McGredy peers over his shoulder at Kent who waits impatiently while watching his back-trail and the valley below.

"You okay back there, kid?"

"All's fine, but I'm not turning back."

McGredy nods and hollers toward Elkman.

"Kid says he ain't turning back!"

Elkman stares at the scant stretch of ground between the forefeet of his horse and the narrow leap to the continuation of the trail on the other side. He curses under his breath and calls out over his shoulder.

"If'n you have any space to untie them animals, you kin drive 'em across."

With a wide-eyed grunt, McGredy looks down at the steep escarpment of rock, scrub, and the valley below.

"Hell, I don't even have 'nough room to dismount let alone ride two abreast unhitchin' skittish stock."

Elkman chokes up on his reins and holds a firm grip on the thick lead rope. He yells back over his shoulder.

"Tell that youngster to grab a fist-full of mane, hold tight and sink spur. We ain't stoppin' till we're all on the other side!"

McGredy calls out behind him to Kent.

"We're gonna charge 'em through . . . if'n they tumble, dismount 'em on the uphill!"

Elkman holds the trailing lead-rope near the knot at the end and lets out the slack. He turns back again to McGredy and nods.

"All set?"

"Ready when you are!"

Nudging his spurred heels, Elkman gives off a charging yowl as he urges his horse and tugs at the trailing string of animals.

"Let's git . . . Yeeouhwee!"

Rocks skitter and tumble as the unshod hooves of the four-legged beasts cut into the eroded path and kick it away. In the short distance to the wash-out, Elkman gives another howling urge at his mount and tugs firm on the lead rope. He hunkers down to jump the carved out abyss and the horses charge forward with muscles flexed, ready to attempt the leap.

The remaining animals left behind with McGredy and Kent get eager and restless at being separated from their companions and drive forward. Crowded at the head of the bunch, McGredy smashes his hat down on his head and jabs his heels.

"Let's go, kid . . . ain't no stoppin' 'em now!"

McGredy charges ahead with snorting steeds pushing at his flank. He turns the corner and watches ahead as Elkman leaps his mount and pack animal across. The five horses in tow, after the pack animal, each hurdle over the void like sheep out to pasture. As the trail abruptly ends at the washout, McGredy braces himself in the saddle and bellows.

"Son of a . . . !"

The excited animals dash forward and down a steepening grade until Elkman gains a foothold and slows the charging horses. He looks back at McGredy, coming on, who grins broadly as he turns from ghastly white to a flushed red-like devil. Elkman holds up the capering horses as he gathers the slack from the lead rope.

"Where's the kid?"

McGredy spins in the saddle and looks behind at the blind turn.

"He was just on my heels 'fore I did that Pegasus jump."

"Well, he ain't there now."

The two wait and listen a moment until the sound of several horses sliding on the rocky trail comes along behind them. Kent rounds the corner at a controlled pace and holds up at the hindmost of McGredy's animals.

"What're you fellers waiting for?"

McGredy exchanges a look with Elkman and shrugs.

"We was just discussin' how getting ten animals up to yer uncle in Montanee warn't too bad a job."

Kent stares at McGredy and jeers.

"If you can leap yer wide-rump across that washout, I sure as shootin' can do it!"

"Yer lucky there's no place for me to dismount and kick your boney-ass back up this mountain."

Elkman laughs quietly and ushers his horses down the trail.

"Yous both can compare backsides later. Let's keep movin' so we can reach that lower valley b'fore dark."

The three riders continue on in their prior ranks, guiding the trailing horse stock down the ever-winding path to less dangerous footing below.

Along the descent, the mountain access path widens and McGredy rides past to the lead position, scanning the trail ahead. Elkman looks at him curiously and rides closer.

"What is it McGredy?"

McGredy hands over the lead rope for his animal string to Elkman.

"Here, hold this, I'm gonna check it out."

Elkman and Kent watch as McGredy rides forward. The solitary rider lopes down into the valley toward a grouping of pines and dismounts. The others continue on and watch from a distance as the former military scout paces the area and takes a knee to study the ground.

The two horseback cowboys steer toward the trees and ride up on the sheltered area. They sit their horses and wait for McGredy's experienced assessment. Finally, Kent speaks up.

"What is it, Indians?"

McGredy walks over leading his mount and peers up at the riders.

"Damn, I knew it."

He shakes his head and intuitively looks over his shoulder as he rests his palm on the handle of his sidearm.

"Ain't Indian markings. These are shod trackings alongside heeled boots."

Elkman scans the ground over and sees faint imprints of hooves in the grassy area.

"How many of them are there?"

"There's a few more than a pair."

McGredy looks at Kent with a scolding glance. The young man sits straight in the saddle, flushed with rising nerves.

"Maybe the two I met weren't with this grouping."

McGredy shrugs and runs his leather reins through his fingers.

"Could be, I guess. I didn't see any obvious tracks or markings coming over that pass. With all that narrow rock, nothing much to show sign."

Elkman looks to the mountains behind them and the high country still ahead.

"Foolin' ourselves won't keep our hides clear."

He looks down at McGredy.

"Can you make a guess to how many were here?"

"I'd say 'bout four or five riders."

Kent watches as Elkman moves his horse over to the grassy area, leaving slack in the lead ropes to let the animals graze. McGredy stands and passes the toe of his boot over the trampled grass.

"What do ya make from it, Tomas?"

"'Bout what I figured."

McGredy looks to Kent then back at Elkman.

"How's that?"

"Leaving two behind to make sure they didn't lose our trail. The kid just rode into their lookouts t'other night most likely."

McGredy walks around his horse and steps up into the saddle. He trots over and takes his string of horses from Elkman. Kent looks back to the trail behind, then ahead.

"What are we going to do?"

Elkman glances over at him questioningly. "How do you mean?"

"If they're ahead of us with two following, we can't just ride into an ambuscade."

McGredy shifts around the saddle seat and lifts his pistol in the holster to keep it from settling too low.

"You jest sit yer horse, boy, and follow what we tell ya, when we tell ya. Like you said, we ain't turnin' 'round."

Kent looks back toward the mountains again.

"We should git some help."

Elkman sniffs as he wipes a gloved finger alongside his nose.

"Out here you're responsible for yerself. Away from civilization, you're the only one to settle right from wrong. We don't know of these fellers' intentions, and until we do, we continue on as before with a watchful eye."

McGredy snorts and aims his horse north.

"We're about to come into Indian Territory. These tagalong riders might yet be the least of our concerns."

Elkman rides ahead with McGredy as they lead the horses along. Sensing the young man's hesitation, Elkman looks back and calls over his shoulder to Kent.

"You gonna be coming along with us?"

"Yes, sir."

"Alright then, keep yer eyes clear."

McGredy curls his lower lip and chin whiskers into his mouth and glances toward Elkman.

"I don't like this any mor'n that kid does."

Elkman nods and continues on.

"Don't see much good comin' from it."

They urge their animals forward, trotting in a tight, watchful group of man and horse through the open valley. To the west over the continental divide, damp clouds of moisture descend into a darkening sky.

Chapter 22

Heavy clouds move across the horizon with the wet smell of rain in the breeze. Late in the afternoon, the three men pile their gear in a protective circle. They stare toward the camp center and the evident lack of a fire. Kent unties his blanket from his rig and pulls it around his shoulders to keep off the cold from the chilling wind. He looks to the others and shivers.

"Smells like we're gonna get rain tonight. Should at least keep those rustler types bedded down."

Elkman pulls the wind-blown brim of his hat down and digs through his saddle bag.

"Depends what caliber they might be."

The cold blustery gale picks up in velocity and McGredy tucks his hat under the corner of his saddle on the ground. He drapes his blanket over his head like a prairie woman's bonnet and pokes his nose out. The wind continues to blow while McGredy shields his face from the coming storm as he speaks.

"Any thief worth his salt would be working in foul weather so his tracks will be covered shortly after."

Tucked down against the seat of his saddle, Elkman nods in agreement toward McGredy. They both turn and watch Kent get situated. The young cowboy holds his blanket tight and, like a dog circling for his spot, curls up against his upended gear using it as a windbreak. Elkman fingers in his vest for his tobacco fixings and voices to no one in particular.

"Keep all yer stuff together. If'n it starts to rain we'll be on our way in the night. Should wash any undesirables from our trail and keep the horses from spookin' 'nd runnin' scatter."

Hunkering down, McGredy repositions his hat under his saddle gear so it won't get too squashed and looks over to Kent, then Elkman.

"Who's gonna keep a lookout."

Elkman licks the wrapping paper of his rolled smoke, glancing up.

"I'll stay awake awhile till full dark. Git some sleep."

Kent tucks himself in a tighter ball and curls behind his saddle.

"Cain't imagine anyone wantin' to steal horses in these conditions."

Elkman carefully lights his short hand-rolled behind his saddle seat and lets a puff of smoke strain through his mustache.

"Surprisin' how sometimes a thief will work harder than an honest man."

McGredy grunts as he lies down to rest.

"Ain't the work they're after always . . . it's the challenge."

Elkman watches his trail partners settle in and quickly pass to slumber. Alert and surveilling the ever-darkening evening sky, the lone cowboy smokes while he lets his eyes wander across the landscape. His sharp steady gaze watches for anything not bedded down in the imminent foul weather.

Rain pours down in gusting sheets through occasional flashes of lightning and thunderclaps. The herd of tethered horses pound hooves and stomp uneasily. Underfoot, the soaking ground churns to mud and they send whickering calls into the night. Through the darkness, a figure throws a saddle on a horse standing separate from the others and fastens it down.

A dull flash of lightning in the distance shows splashes of water bouncing off leather saddle skirting from a rig on the ground. The figure next to it, lying covered in a water-glistened wool blanket, rolls over sensing a presence overhead and peeks out. Kent looks up to see Elkman standing above him as another flash of lightning pops nearby. Several seconds pass before the growl of thunder rumbles through the blackness. Elkman wipes the rain from his face and flicks it aside.

"Pack it up, we're leaving."

Kent looks up through the pouring rain and winces as the drops splash into his eyes.

"What time is it?"

"Time to git moving."

Kent shakes off his wet covering and pulls on his sodden cowboy hat. He stands and wrings out the soaking blanket while his eyes adjust in the night. Across the washed out camp, Kent watches McGredy as he wipes his hand over wet horsehide before throwing his blanket and rig on his mount. The wind blows cold and damp and Kent peers down at his own gear while puddles of water start to surround the mound of leather and rawhide.

The rainy downpour continues as the three riders lead the glossy-wet string of horses. Drops of rainwater splash the puddle-soaked ground and the parade of muddy hooves slosh and churn the earthen trail. There is an electric tinge in the air that clings between the thunderstorms looming in the mountains and treetops. The light of daybreak is masked by heavy clouds, leaving a damp and dreary gray morning.

Kent rides up next to Elkman and gives a soaked shudder. He watches the veteran cowboy as he rides on, determined and steady, unflinching in the harsh bone-drenching conditions.

"We gonna stop anytime soon?"

Elkman looks to the gloomy skies to the west and north.

"Doesn't look that way."

"We rode all night. Shouldn't we rest during the day?"

Elkman pulls at his collar to keep the cold, chilled rain from his neck. He glances at Kent and continues riding.

"Don't know yer situation, but I'm soaked to the saddle. Sitting fer a nap this way just don't seem all that appealing."

"We can't just keep going all day while it rains."

Elkman snuffles and wipes the mist of rain from his mustache.

"You'd be surprised how far you'll get."

The day wears on as the sky continues to hang in a gray haze of moisture. Occasional showers of rain burst from the sky sending a cold nip of agony into the already soaked horsemen. Through the drizzle, the sky begins to darken again and the shelter of a small parcel of trees looks inviting to the weary riders.

Elkman navigates toward the patch of woods, studies it briefly, and dismounts. He turns to the others as they rein up.

"We'll sleep here tonight."

McGredy gives a cold shudder and slides from the saddle with his coiled rope in hand. With cold stiff hands, he lashes one end around a tree to form a picket line.

Still horseback, Kent drops the lead line and steers his mount over to a pile of brush. He steps down from the saddle and lifts the vegetation looking for dry tinder underneath. Unhitching the wet leather cinch,

Elkman pulls his saddle and places it on a damp clump of grass. He lays his blanket over top and notices Kent's attempt to gather firewood.

"No need to be lookin' for lumber."

"Why is that?"

"We just traveled all night and day. Would be kinder pointless to send up a signal to our whereabouts now."

Kent holds several partially dry sticks in hand. He looks at them with downcast eyes, feeling miserable, cold, and wet.

"I have to get dried out. My bones and skin feel like the rot's gonna set in."

McGredy chimes in as he ties off the other end of the picket line.

"Ain't like the ranch hereabouts, where ya got a nice stove to sit around in the evenin'."

Kent gives a feeble glare to McGredy and watches Elkman unbridle his mount. Elkman looks up through the scant shelter of the pines and sniffs the air.

"Yer outfit ain't gonna dry by morning. Besides, it's fixin' to rain again soon. Jest take care of yer horse 'nd rest yerself."

The young man drops the potential camp-wood and moves around his horse and unsaddles. He watches McGredy finish with his horses at the picket line and take his blanket to a low shrub which he proceeds to crawl under. With his wet blanket in hand, Kent looks around bemused.

"Who's gonna stand watch tonight?"

Elkman lifts the low branches of another small pine and looks for a partially sheltered spot to keep off the weather.

"No one is."

He kicks away some of the damp mulch under the tree and finds semi-dry ground. Nearby, McGredy pokes out from his blanket.

"They'd have tried to steal our stock in the night if the occasion arose. You'd a'woke near warm but shy any horses."

Kent stands alone in the continuing haze of drizzle and looks between the two men hiding away like animals for winter.

"What about tonight?"

McGredy grumbles.

"They'll wait till the weather clears some before tracking for us again."

"You don't think they followed us?"

Elkman sets his hat aside and pulls his blanket up over his head.

"If you had a choice, would you?"

The young cowboy looks over to the picketed horses as they slumber, eyes half-shut with rivulets of water running off their rain-soaked hides. He gives an uncontrolled shudder then shakes out his damp blanket and tries to find a sheltered spot away from the surrounding wetness.

Chapter 23

The sky at the break of dawn is dark as the rain pours heavy and rolls of thunder rumble in the distance. In the cold, dreary light, Elkman and McGredy are up moving around with streams of water rolling off the edges of their wide brimmed hats. McGredy looks down at Kent who is still curled in a ball, sleeping. The boy trembles occasionally but remains quiet.

"Should we wake him or jest leave 'em for a gully washer to take care of?"

"We leave 'em and you'd have to do his share of the job."

"Aww, bring 'em along then, it's nice to have someone to bark at when I get cranky."

McGredy gives a shiver at his clothes hanging soaked and cold to his large frame.

"I'm more of a town sleeper and this dampness is starting to chap my hide."

"I ain't enjoin' it much, 'cept to watch you whimper."

McGredy smirks at Elkman through the steady drizzle.

"I do have to hand it to the kid, he don't complain much. That's the thing 'bout not knowing any better . . . that kid just treats everything like another day of work."

Elkman smiles from under his drenched floppy brim and walks over to Kent. He gives the young cowboy a few taps of his soggy boot toe until he stirs Kent awake.

"Hey kid, we're moving out."

Kent rolls over and opens his blanket to peek out, letting the rain bounce off his face.

"We still have the horses?"

"Yep, looks as if we'll have to keep going."

Kent seems only partly relieved at the news of the horses not being stolen as he nods, staring skyward. Elkman takes a step away then turns. He wipes the back of his hand across his wet chin and gestures to McGredy saddling a horse.

"McGredy is ill-tempered and ready to git, so hop to it."

"When ain't he in a sour mood?"

"Whenever his playing card deck ain't in danger of getting' soaked he's in pretty good spirits."

Kent drops the blanket to his shoulders.

"Hope he's better at cards than cowboyin'."

Elkman glances at McGredy, sees he's not listening, and grins.

"He is that."

The rain continues steadily as Elkman walks to his wet gear to begin saddling. Kent rises and shakes the water from his sopping blanket. The young cowboy stands in the pouring rain and quietly watches the two men near the group of tethered horses. Smiling to himself, he leans down and grabs his damp hat from under the brush. Slapping it on his leg, he looks to the cloud-heavy sky and lets the deluge wash over him. The raindrops splash on his face and he hollers to the heavens.

"Let's drive 'em north, boys!"

Elkman and McGredy look over at Kent and then to each other in an exchange of amused looks. They slowly break into laughter at their miserable rain-soaked situation. The young innocent's call to action relieves the tension for a moment of liberated acceptance while the torrential downpour continues to drench them from head to foot.

The three horsemen ride north through wide, open terrain with the mountains to their left and push on, only occasionally scanning the back trail. The rain has stopped for the moment, but the overcast clouds and cold wind make for a miserable day. The three strings of horses follow in line—cold, damp, and somber.

McGredy urges his horse up alongside Elkman in the lead and adjusts himself in the saddle apprehensively. Elkman notices his anxiety and looks around for possible signs of concern.

"What is it, McGredy?"

"If we keep along this trail, we'll come up on a broken down burg called Twin Fork Gulch. I've been through it a time or two and I think it'd be best to avoid it with this abundance of saleable horse flesh we're packin'."

Kent brings his horses up to hear what the weather-soaked pair is speaking about. McGredy gives him a sidelong glance then continues.

"I've been thinking it's probably where those men were headed. Would surely explain why the kid got that bad feelin' 'bout them."

Elkman scans the isolated surroundings, the swath of a trail they've found themselves following, and nods.

"Alright, if'n you think it best."

Kent eases his horse closer and turns to Elkman.

"What's going on?"

Riding between the two opposites of character, Elkman looks at McGredy then Kent.

"We're gonna head a bit further east for a day or so to avoid a possible town up yonder."

Cold, wet, and instantly irritable, Kent puts on a hissy attitude.

"Another day or so? We want to get these horses north the quickest route possible before them trailing rustlers or Indians catch up with us."

McGredy maneuvers his mount forward to see Kent clear and roars past Elkman toward him.

"Ya damned greenhorn, if either of 'em know we're here, there's no question 'bout 'em catching up." With a snort, McGredy lets his horse drift back so he doesn't have to look at Kent.

The young cowboy bristles and shakes his head. "What the hell would you know . . ."

Elkman twirls the tail end of his lead rope and gives it a slap on the leg of Kent's chaps.

"Understand this kid. McGredy knows a lot of the behaviors 'round these parts. If *he* says go around else there'll be trouble, you go around at double arms-length."

Elkman adjusts his hat, looks at McGredy then back at Kent.

"I'm sorry we cain't afford to help you learn the hard way on this one. Take it from a fella who has and trust me."

Kent smirks.

"Do I have a choice?"

"You always have a choice."

Elkman grins and gives his horse a tap with his spurs.

"These here horses don't though."

Elkman steers them from their traveled path and heads to the east, veering from the marks of a natural trail ahead. McGredy rides along and sits high in the saddle watching for signs of settlement to the north. He calls out to Elkman as he follows east.

"I'll be damned if I ever made efforts to ride clear of a gamblin' town before."

Elkman looks back at McGredy over his shoulder.

"Yer jest making the best wager for gettin' yer hide north."

Reluctantly following with his string of stock, Kent pulls up his collar tight at his neck to repel the constant wet and cold.

Chapter 24

With damp blankets wrapped around their bodies, the three horsemen sit around a small campfire. In the last glow of afternoon light, a slight steam of mist rises off the woolen covering as McGredy sits closer to the short flames. He peers up at the others and grunts, laughing slightly.

"Damn, we're sitting like three shiverin' Injuns around this pitiful flame. You know the difference between them and us?"

Elkman raises an eye at the comment and lays his wet gloves on his crossed knees trying to get some dry into them. "What's that?"

"Injuns make small fires and sit close while whites make big fires and sit far."

Kent thinks a moment and half smiles at McGredy.

"I could sure use a big fire and would still sit close."

McGredy nods toward the young man.

"Might got some Injun ways in ya."

The kid shoots an amused look toward McGredy for the first time and their acrimony seems to fade over mutual suffering. McGredy pats his sodden vest under his wet coat.

"Damn . . . near everything I own is damp and musty . . . and nearly froze."

Elkman works his cold fingers near the minimal heat.

"Could be the weather'll be clearer tomorrow. Be able to dry a few things out if it does."

Kent sits quietly shivering and McGredy scratches under his beard at his neck.

"A little sunshine would do wonder for my undergarments. I'm soaked near clean through 'nd my skin's wrinkled up like a hog's neck in wintertime."

Shaking off the cold, McGredy unbuttons his vest and feels the dampness underneath. Kent works another slightly dry stick on the small fire and the wet cowboys stare into the smoking flame as the evening sky fades to the dark of night.

The chilly morning reveals itself to be continuing gray and cloudy with mists of rain. The three cowboys lead the trailing horse stock and ride along, their saddle mounts abreast, visibly damp with souring spirits. None of the riders utter a word as they move in a long arc to the east and then travel north.

As they veer back slightly to the west, Kent looks to the skies and notices a spot of blue trying to break through. He turns in the saddle to McGredy and watches him ride, wet and sullen. The young cowboy aims his attentions toward Elkman as he eagerly points to the sky and smiles.

"Might be we'll end up with a touch of sunshine on us."

Elkman nods and continues riding. McGredy moves his horse up next to Elkman and grunts. "He sure do get excited about a brief glimpse of sky."

Elkman glances up to the clouds overhead.

"It may clear yet."

"Not soon 'nough. My wet ass is as craggy as an old woman's gobbler."

Elkman stares at McGredy and winces at his crass comment. He watches the somber gambler a moment then speaks.

"One thing good 'bout this weather is it don't encourage you to make a lot of conversation."

"Oh, I've been doin' a lot of thinking . . . it'll come out sooner or later."

Crinkling his brow, Elkman continues on silently and adjusts his own wet britches against the soaked leather seat of the saddle.

The path of travel continues toward the north and west and the procession of horseback riders keeps on. The weather has cleared mostly to bright skies as have the dark moods. Along with the warming sun, spots of dry appear on their clothing and the color begins to return to their flesh. Elkman leads the group to the edge of an escarpment and waits while the others move up.

Perched horseback, surveying from the ridge, the three observe the ordinarily dry gully running with rainwater nearly twenty feet across. They scan the length of the wash looking for the safest place to cross. Elkman points to a spot just after the bend where it appears to widen out shallow with less current.

"That spot'll do, beyond the narrows. Might as well dry out our things on the other side."

McGredy shrugs.

"Looks like as good a place to cross as any."

"I'll take point and lead 'em across. If'n they have to swim, point 'em down current to the opposite shore."

Kent huffs and murmurs quiet.

"I've crossed rivers 'fore."

Elkman leans down on his saddle horn and glances over at Kent.

"This ain't a river and won't act the part. A gully-washer could quit at any time or double in size. Jest follow along, point 'em across and they'll end up on the other side most likely."

Kent looks to McGredy alongside him and then to Elkman.

"I'll follow you across jest fine."

Elkman observes the short moment of nonaggressive behavior and backs his horse away from the overhanging ridge. He rides his mount along the rocky bank a quarter mile then maneuvers his horse and string of animals down the embankment into the rushing current.

The horses towed onward, they leap and plunge into the cold muddy water. Not wanting to misstep on the eroded shore, McGredy is quick to follow into the swift waters. He makes use of the herd behavior and the tendency of the horses wanting to stick together as he crowds behind the other splashing animals. He wades into deeper water and nearly slips from the saddle as his horse bucks in the chest-high current.

In a splash of mane and tail, Kent follows with his trailing animals into the flowing gully. Halfway across the wash, Elkman slogs with his horses neck-deep. The mount Elkman sits astride suddenly drops from sight a moment before kicking off the rocky bottom and paddling across, nostrils flared and spitting water. The connected string of led animals follows behind in perfect formation, wide-eyed on the swimming horse before them.

Wet from heels to hat, Elkman comes ashore the other side and scampers his string of animals up the steep rocky grade. He circles them at the top of the embankment and watches as McGredy leads his horses out of the gully with young Kent close behind. They gather at the overlook above the rushing waters. Elkman looks over his companions, drenched once again and washed through.

"We can hold up here a bit 'nd dry out."

McGredy nods and feels for the wet coins and folding money in his vest pocket. He gives them a comforting pat.

"Sounds like a good idea. I've some items to tend to."

Kent scans the hilly surroundings and appears apprehensive.

"How long are we gonna hold up?

McGredy shoots him a sour look.

"Till I'm good and ready. That a problem for ya?"

Kent stares out to the landscape and the warmth of the afternoon sun fails to comfort the young man's uneasiness.

"I'm just wondering 'bout them fellas tracking us?"

Following Kent's gaze, Elkman adjusts his hat and turns to McGredy, who looks around unconcerned.

"What'd you figure, McGredy?"

McGredy grips his shirt sleeve in a fist and wrings it out.

"I guess we should be clear of them most likely. That den of thieves. Twin Fork Gulch is a day's ride west o' here. They probably figure us headed for Kansas 'nd not worth the trouble."

The young cowboy looks to the satisfied reassurance of Elkman which relaxes him somewhat.

"If ya don't think they're following? I *could* use a wash."

McGredy grunts and wrings out his other sleeve.

"Hell, we've been getting a wash for the last few days. I could use a dry."

Elkman unties his kerchief and lets it hang loose around his neck.

"Catching a spell of dryness it is . . ."

Elkman turns his horse, prods the animal and rides a short distance away from the gully toward a clear patch in the brush. He lets the lead rope fall so the string of horses can graze and he rides the perimeter looking for human mark or trail. McGredy lets his horses gather with the others and checks for markings further out.

Both men satisfied with the lack of sign, Elkman glances to the broken sun in the sky, dismounts, and goes to unsaddling. The others follow over, step down from their horses, and begin pulling their soaked gear. With the water-logged leather of saddles and tack spread on the ground along with draped damp blankets over brush and limb, the camp looks like it was formed by an explosion of trappings.

Elkman and Kent, stripped of their outer coat layers, start assembling a fire as McGredy peels off his wet vest. McGredy continues to pull his soaked shirt over his head and walks around with his long-handle underwear exposed as he drapes his wet articles of clothing on low tree branches. Elkman lights the fire and looks to his nearby water canteen.

"Probably should fill up my drinkin' reserves 'fore McGredy takes a dip in that stream."

McGredy pulls off one of his boots and throws it to the side.

"Best do it quick, cause I'm about to do my underclothes laundry too."

Elkman tosses another branch on the small flames of the campfire and stands. He unbuttons his vest, empties the pockets and drops it over his saddle horn.

"Ya gonna wash while wearin' or do it like a Chinaman?"

McGredy rocks back tugging at his other boot.

"I haven't skinned these britches in so long, it's gonna take a swift current to git 'em off me."

Elkman sits and leans back to slip off his boots and strip his worn wool socks. Kent watches the two grown men peeling layers of clothing without any sense of modesty. He handles and shapes his damp felt hat and lays it aside as he watches the two other men in their long-johns. Kent thinks a moment, grabs up his canteen, and runs toward the river holding the container high.

"I'm gonna fill up my drinkin' jug before either of you get near that gully with yer filthy washing!"

In an air of relieved moods, Elkman and McGredy run barefoot in their trousers and undershirts following Kent, whooping it up and swinging their wooden canteens overhead.

At the edge of the arroyo, Kent stands at the top of the embankment and looks to the swirl of water below. He looks behind at the two half-dressed cowboys charging toward him and back again to the steep decline. Pausing just a moment, Kent slides down the rocky bluff into the swirling pool of rainwater several feet down.

In quick succession, Elkman and McGredy come running over the edge and plunge into the gully with a splash. McGredy comes to the surface first and splashes toward Kent.

"There ya go, kid!"

Kent slogs away through the waist deep current to fill his canteen as Elkman lies back in the cool water and looks up to the clearing blue skies. The men scrub and swim in the small breakwater off the main gulch like youngsters washing away the cares of the world.

Chapter 25

The three washed cowboys bask in the sun, lounging around the campfire in their long-johns with their clothing scattered to every surrounding twig and branch. Elkman enjoys a shop-rolled cigar as he lies back on the warming ground. McGredy feels his socks for dampness and drapes them over a stick pushed upright in the ground near the fire.

"Everything I own is soaked through. How'd you manage a dry cigar?"

Elkman takes a puff and smiles. "Priorities."

Kent leans back on his elbows and fingers a hole in the belly of his underwear shirt.

"What are you two planning on doing after we get these horses north?"

Elkman coughs as he blows a smoke ring skyward.

"McGredy is planning on getting hitched."

"The hell I am! Just plan on doing some visiting." McGredy shoots Elkman a scolding glance. "How dare you accuse me of matrimonial aspirations?"

Kent chuckles at the comment as McGredy ceases his pacing and sits down near the fire. Their aggression toward each other has seemed to wane for a short time. The large gambler eyes Kent's frayed and under-sized long-handles.

"I speculate young Kent here figures on buying some new undergarments."

McGredy smirks as Kent pulls his finger from the worn shirt hole.

"What do you plan on doing, Mister Tomas H. Elkman?"

They both look to Elkman lounged back in his worn and stained underwear. He remains silent as he relaxes with his hat pushed back on his head, having a smoke and satisfied with life. McGredy wriggles his toes and brushes the sandy grit off the bottoms. He grins mischievously toward Elkman.

"You're the one gonna end up with all this money in yer pocket with no place to put it. Ye already got a horse, a saddle, 'nd a hat. If anything, yer the fella most likely to end up getting' attached. Women kin smell newly acquired wealth like a skunk in a chicken house."

Elkman takes the cigar from his teeth, looks at the chewed butt of his smoke and shrugs.

"Gettin' tethered ain't something that bodes well for me."

He glances up at McGredy who gives him a sly knowing look. The observant gambler winks and tilts his head toward their young trail partner.

"Ain't thinkin' of tagging 'long with young Kent here back to that ranch in Colorado?"

Elkman ignores McGredy's comment, tosses the remainder of the cigar in the fire, and feels one of his boots for dryness. Kent perks at the mention of his family ranch.

"I ain't headed back right quick. Figured I'd spend some time with my kin in Montana a spell."

McGredy nods reassuringly.

"Good for you kid. No sense in turning 'round and heading back after all the time ya took gettin' there."

The young cowboy looks to Elkman, interested.

"Mister Elkman, you thinking 'bout heading back there?"

"Guess I'll check out the territory some and move on."

Kent sits up and brushes off his elbows.

"Move on to where?"

"O'er them mountains to the west, probably. Seems the more I travel, the more I haven't seen."

Giving a short laugh, McGredy tosses wood on the warming fire.

"Ya see kid, this here man is a true drifter . . . wandering the territory, enriching the lives of you and me then moving on, never to settle down and experience true happiness for hisself."

Elkman crinkles his forehead and grunts.

"Where'd you come up with that load of horse-dung? I just haven't found a place I feel comfortable staying at for long."

The sun breaks through a cloud and Kent speaks up.

"Maybe you just need a good woman."

Both Elkman and McGredy break into amused laughter and Kent blurts out, offended. "What's so funny?"

Elkman looks at the disconcerted youth sitting awkwardly, embarrassed. He tosses a stick on the fire and glances up at McGredy and Kent.

"There are good women out there, but not many west of the Mississippi. 'Sides, why make one woman miserable for the rest of her life when I can make a hundred happy for the rest of mine?"

McGredy nods his approval with a broad smile.

"Ya should probably stick to that, although once you catch a whiff of Miss Kay's friends you might change yer tune."

Elkman grins as he pulls on his dry trousers.

"Anything's possible when it comes to them sort."

Interested and excited, Kent leans forward.

"Does Miss Kay have any friends that might be my brand?" McGredy pretends to think quietly a moment.

"No."

"Why?"

"These here are real ladies. They'd feel guilty deflowering a scrappy colt like yerself."

Kent sits straight and looks to Elkman then McGredy, trying to hide his humiliation.

"I've been with plenty of women."

McGredy throws a broad wink toward Elkman.

"Sure ya have, kid."

The young cowboy jumps to his feet and advances toward McGredy, not sure what he wants to do. He stands across the campfire from the large beaming gambler and clenches his fist. Elkman takes his boots and half-heartedly raises them to block Kent's path to McGredy.

"Easy there kid. You git mixed up with McGredy here and you might not get another chance at the young gals."

McGredy looks up at Kent and shakes his head as he lies back, smoothing his hands through his thick, dark hair.

"I know all about young pups like yerself trying hard to prove you're grown men. Hell, most the barroom gunfights and fracases I seen stem from yer sort."

"Damn you anyway, McGredy, what do you know?"

Elkman wriggles his toes into a wool sock and feels his toes at the end. He shakes out one of his tall boots and tucks his trouser leg as he pulls it on. He glances up at Kent as the young man steps away in a pouting sulk to check his clothing's wetness.

"When it comes to them type of gals, I bet Jefferson there knows more'n you'll want to ever find out."

McGredy smiles and thrusts his hips at Kent repeatedly.

"That's right. Maybe I'll find ya an old broken down heifer to teach ya the basics. She'll need the work and you'll be happy for the lesson."

Finished pulling on his other boot, Elkman stands and tosses a stick of wood toward McGredy who still lies on his back gyrating his hips.

"See'ng ya dance on the bar once in my life is enough. Let's pack camp 'nd get movin' a few hours 'fore evening sets in."

Taking his dried shirt from a branch, Elkman slips into the pullover garment while Kent tugs at his boot straps. McGredy feels his hanging pants for dryness and adjusts himself into his britches.

Elkman picks up a wooden canteen next to his gear, takes a swig, and pours the remainder on the coals of the fire. He tosses the empty canteen to Kent's blanket.

"Kent, dump yer jug on these coals and refill 'em with fresh water will ya?"

Kent stares silently at Elkman briefly and slowly senses his obligation of duty to the more experienced cowboy. He empties his own canteen on the dying fire and grabs up the other canteen to be filled. Elkman gives Kent a knowing nod.

"Thanks . . . you ain't half as bad as McGredy always grumbles about."

Kent stares over at McGredy and grabs at his groin.

"Hey McGredy, ya want me to fill yer water too?"

The gambler gives his canteen a swish and drops it to his pile of gear. "I'll pass on that offer, thank ye very much."

McGredy spreads open his unfastened britches and turns to relieve himself on the bushes nearby.

"I was just thinkin' of toppin' yers but my stream is so full of old whiskey you'd be hard set to ride yer horse."

Elkman shakes out his saddle blanket and lays it over his trappings.

"Well, keep yer squirtin' pecker away from that fire or you'll have the camp up in flames."

Kent laughs as he hangs Elkman's canteen strap over his shoulder and carries both containers down toward the gully. McGredy finishes his business and watches Kent disappear over the ridge toward the water's edge. He exchanges an approving look with Elkman and they resume packing their gear.

Chapter 26

The once rushing water of the gully now flows easy and gentle. Kent looks down the lazily meandering stream at the crumbling rock banks carved from the massive surge of rainwater. The young cowboy slides down to the water's edge, kneels next to the passing current and uncorks the canteens. He submerges both the wooden containers, watching as air bubbles burst from the openings, and listens to the chugging sounds of liquid pushing in.

Suddenly a rifle shot rings out and Kent is pushed back to the embankment. He looks across the gully to a puff of black powder smoke rising from the brush and then down to the dark discoloring on his shirt. A delayed shock of pain pulses through him as he releases the canteens and clutches his bloody abdomen.

Standing by the dwindling smolder of the fire, Elkman and McGredy stop and turn at the sound of the gunshot.

"Sounded like a rifle . . ."

As the words leave McGredy's lips he looks to the Winchester propped up against Kent's saddle. They both immediately jump to action, Elkman grabbing up his pistol belt and rifle and McGredy grabbing Kent's long-gun.

Another shot rings out and Kent's body jolts again. Blood begins to come to his lips as he tries to call for help. Writhing in agony, the young cowboy digs his heels into the muddy bank and tries to push himself to cover. His eyes move upward toward the top of the ridge where the outlines of Elkman and McGredy suddenly appear.

McGredy shoulders the rifle, snapping off several shots into the opposite bank as Elkman hops the ridge and slides down the embankment to Kent's side. Rocks and sand tumble in his path as he scoots to the aid of the wounded companion. His pistol in hand, Elkman lays his rifle and holster aside and pulls Kent into his arms. "Hold on kid, we're here . . ."

From above, McGredy leaps to the water and continues firing the rifle. Several gunshots snap from the opposite bank and Elkman fires his long sighted pistol at the faintest glimpse of a target. McGredy levers the rifle empty and stumbles back out of the water toward the shore. With Kent still embraced in his arms, Elkman grabs up his rifle and holds it out for McGredy.

"Here! Jefferson, take this."

McGredy drops Kent's rifle to the embankment and takes up Elkman's '73 Winchester. He fires repeatedly, working the lever action as several shooters scramble away on the opposing sandbar. A splash further downstream catches both their attention. Elkman reloads his six-shot pistol and calls out.

"McGredy, the horses!"

They watch helpless as all fifteen horses as well as their own saddle mounts and pack animal are herded across the gully. McGredy raises the rifle and fires to no effect. He levers the rifle again, takes careful aim, and shoots a long clear shot at one of the horseback rustlers, dropping him from the saddle into the stream.

There is movement across the river and Elkman fires his pistol at the fleeing assassins on the opposite bank until his pistol clicks empty again on a spent chamber. He watches them disappear over the ridge out of sight as McGredy snaps off several more shots at the horseback thieves.

Hesitant and slowly lowering the rifle, McGredy scans the lonely mud-splashed gulch and lets his eyes drop to the passing current. He waits for more gunfire, but none comes through the black-powder charged stillness. McGredy stands quiet, not wanting to face the reality of circumstances behind him. He listens to the quiet rush of water at his feet and the youth's fading pants of final breath. Finally, he turns to look at Elkman on the edge of the muddy bank.

Still embracing the young man in his arms, Elkman looks down at the lifeless body, now limp, with several blood-spattered bullet wounds. He looks momentarily at McGredy, then lets his eyes fall to the blood-tinged water rushing by at his feet.

The clear sky seems cruel as it shines brightly over the somber scene of mourning. Elkman stands by a crude grave as McGredy kneels and places the last stone on the pile. They stare quietly at the crossed wooden sticks marking Kent's final resting place. McGredy sits back on his haunches and sighs.

"Damn son . . . ne'er meant to ride 'em so hard. Jest reminded me of a cocky kid I knew back when I became a scout for the Army. Didn't deserve to die that a'way."

Elkman clenches his jaw to check his emotions.

"Could have been any of us."

McGredy stands and dusts off his knees, then turns to Elkman.

"Now what?"

The two stand quietly a moment until Elkman puts on his hat and looks to McGredy stone-faced.

"We go 'nd get the kid's horses back."

McGredy watches as Elkman steps away, grabs up his saddle and hitches it over his shoulder. Walking due west toward Twin Fork Gulch, Elkman sets out at a slow but determined pace. McGredy takes a long final look at young Kent's grave and swallows hard.

"We'll get 'em for ya kid . . . or die tryin'."

Chapter 27

The leather soles and stacked heels of boots scrape across hard ground. Elkman and McGredy carry a weighty burden as they tread toward the mountainous foothills in the west. They continue to trudge on wearily, with sullen demeanor, as they carry their bundled saddles and rifles in hand.

Despite the chill wind, traces of sweat run down their hard faces. A bulging saddlebag draped over his shoulder, McGredy stops and drops his gear before him. He inspects the ground, counting the hoof prints and checking their direction of travel. Elkman stands by and stares stoically forward. The evening dusk comes early behind the mountains and McGredy looks up to the darkening western horizon and grits his teeth.

"That's where they're headed . . . Twin Fork Gulch."

A cold breeze blows over them and Elkman takes in a lungful that burns his insides. He drops his saddle at his feet to rest a moment and rolls his shoulders from the strain.

"What type of place is this Twin Fork Gulch?"

"Last time I was there, didn't stick around much for sightseeing. Chances are when we get there we're going to be terribly out-gunned."

Elkman nods and adjusts his sweat-ringed hat.

"Any kind of law abouts?"

Releasing a sigh of fatigue, McGredy thinks.

"I didn't run into any, but I tend to avoid such things. There might be some around, but since the gold ran out, that place is just a hole of leftovers and a nest of hired guns and thieves."

The two regain their breath while adjusting their coats against the cold. Hacking a lump of phlegm from his heaving chest, McGredy shrugs.

"Was more'n a few years ago that I passed through. Maybe it's different now. One of the big buildings in town had sunk into the ground. Hell, could be the whole place is swallowed up now."

Elkman reaches down and picks up his saddle.

"Well, that's where we're headed so we'll find out soon 'nough. We can walk through the night and hit 'em early."

McGredy grabs up his saddle and follows.

"We should be there by breakfast . . ."

A cold mist of pre-morning hangs in the air, casting an ominous haze of light over the mountains. The ground fog begins to burn away with the early light as Elkman and McGredy appear to rise from the landscape. They walk slow and determined, as they crest the hill on their approach toward Twin Fork Gulch.

They drop their saddles behind some shrub covering around an outcropping of rock near the edge of town and hold their rifles at the ready. The two wearied men exchange an accepting look of actions to be taken and walk toward the once bustling mining town. Elkman scans the tall, mostly abandoned paint-chipped structures in town and glances over at McGredy.

"The tracks from all our stock come right through here."

McGredy looks to the markings on the ground and nods.

"Yup, and they ain't too caring 'bout anyone knowing it either. We've been followin' 'em plain through the dark."

They both watch the wide, empty street before them. An older woman crosses with a basket of laundry without looking their way. The predawn fog and emptiness of the street makes the big wood-framed buildings look particularly ominous. Elkman looks past the half dozen horses tied out front of a saloon to a sign for livery at the far end of town.

"Ya think our animals are down at the stables?"

"That's where the trail leads."

"They must know we're coming?"

McGredy grunts. "Doubt if they care."

Adjusting the hold on his Winchester, Elkman scans the street.

"We should hit 'em at the saloon first."

"Figured as much. Less we want them after us again."

McGredy looks down at the rifle in his hands.

"I ain't much of a shot with this."

"Yeah, I noticed."

The burly gambler shoots a sour look toward Elkman as they continue walking into town.

Elkman and McGredy walk the edge of the empty main street, observing the dilapidated buildings as they pass. A few people clad in nightclothes look out from dusty or broken windows to watch the armed strangers travel by afoot. The two determined-looking men with their rifles held at the ready have the distinct look of being on the hunt.

On the easily tracked trail of the horse rustlers, they pass several empty buildings and continue to follow the muddy hoof-prints in the water-puddled street. The sound of banjo playing comes from the saloon with several saddled mounts out front. The music captures their attention and they position themselves with a view of the wide glass-front window.

A burning rage swells inside Elkman as he stares at what he believes to be the murdering horse thieves sitting at the game table inside. He can clearly see two of the men at play and instantly recognizes them from McGredy's hostile encounter at the cards weeks earlier.

The distinct clicking sound of the hammer on a rifle being pulled back snaps Elkman to attention and he turns to see McGredy raising the walnut stock of his long-gun to his shoulder.

"Hold it . . ."

"What fer? You know who them fellers are!"

Elkman holds his hand up to McGredy and glances back over his shoulder toward the saloon.

"We know for sure it's them?"

"I'm sure 'nough."

McGredy moves his rifle's aim around Elkman's raised hand and draws a bead.

"I can take one out from here to start the ball rolling."

"We're gonna need the upper hand."

"Go'n guns blazing and we will have."

"We got to be smart about this. I don't want either of us shot up needless."

Breaking from his stance, McGredy lowers the rifle barrel.

"Do ya have another plan?"

"I noticed something down the street."

Elkman gestures to a building with a lighted oil lamp set back near the livery. He lowers his voice and ushers McGredy to the boardwalk opposite the saloon.

"It's early yet, less sleep and more whiskey won't make 'em any sharper."

Reluctantly lowering the hammer on his rifle, McGredy backs to the boardwalk and follows Elkman further down the street toward the livery. The banjo music resonates in the mostly deserted canyon of buildings and the sound of laughter sends a chilling echo into the morning mist.

Chapter 28

At the far end of town, the forms of Elkman and McGredy can be seen, lamp-lit inside an old dilapidated building with dirty, web-cracked windows and peeling paint. With a groan of timber, the free-standing wood structure appears to have a distinct lean from the erosion under the rot-felled corner of the porch. The broken bullet-ridden sign over the door reads in painted letters: MARSHAL OF HENSON COUNTY.

Slowly, the front door to the building drags open, straining on the hinges. An old, age-ripened Territory Marshal steps out to the boardwalk and peers down the street. He wears a faded broad-brimmed black hat which rests on a head of silvery hair. The deep grooves on his face all trail to the long grey mustache that hangs low over his lip. His dark suit of clothes partly conceals a pair of ivory handled pistols that contrast his time-worn look.

The marshal steps out into the muddy street and a sleepy deputy follows at his heels. The subordinate lawman's age seems to make the marshal look youthful. He walks with a gimpy hobble and carries a sawed off shotgun in the crook of his arm. Whiskered ear to ear and from the eyeballs down, the deputy glances back at the two trail-hands and gives a reassuring nod.

Elkman and McGredy exchange a skeptical look as they follow their newfound assistance outside. McGredy scratches his nose and sniffs cynically as he watches the elderly lawmen stride across the street toward the livery barn.

"We should've let them sleep 'nd took care of it ourselves."

Elkman shrugs toward McGredy.

"Didn't think that deputy would rouse short of a fire."

"What do ya think now of yer plan?"

Elkman carries his rifle and watches.

"Tips the scale a bit."

"For us or them?"

The interior of the saloon has a rough-sawn panel wood bar and at the back of the room and a narrow staircase leading upstairs. Both features of the room are worn dirty with the look of heavy use. The scant décor in the establishment includes an old, soot-covered oil painting of a nude woman that hangs near a wood-burning stove perched in a box of sand and a pair of snowshoes with the rawhide rat-chewed to disrepair.

At a table seated near the front window, the four rustlers play cards and drink house brew from a mismatch of secondhand bottles. Boss Carloff sits next to his two gaming pals along with several soiled doves standing behind. He lays out his hand and looks up to the fourth man. From under a sugarloaf sombrero, the man looks to the faces around the table and slowly smiles a distinct corn-toothed grin.

Bob Snarel splays out his winning cards and gives a raspy chuckle. He rakes in the winnings and pushes his discarded playing hand toward the dealer on his right.

"You boys sure ain't very good at this game."

One of the rustlers stands and grabs a bottle of whiskey. He takes a long swig and adjusts himself inside his trousers.

"You're about as fun to play with as that broad-assed tinhorn gambler McGredy."

Snarel looks up at the cowboy and sneers.

"I got you even with him, didn't I?"

"Yeah, but until we sell them horses, he took most our playin' money and now you're doin' it jest same as he was."

Snarel glances down at the man's hand still scratching away inside his britches. He grimaces as he looks to the occupants at the table.

"Why don't you go outside with that itch? The gals in here sure don't want it."

With a keen eye he studies one of the three sporting girls gathered near the table getting an occasional sip poured in her clutched glass. They exchange a smile and she gives an uncomfortable gaze toward the scratching cowboy. Snarel snorts an angered breath and glares at the itchy offender. The cowboy continues a moment, then stops with his hand still wrist deep and takes another gulp from the bottle.

"I just gots to piss is all. I ain't got the bugs."

The men at the table groan in discord and go back to the cards being dealt around the table. Snarel tosses a few coins to the pot and the others follow. He glances up at the cowboy still standing with his hand employed.

"You gonna piss here or outside?"

The cowboy pauses his scratching and looks to Carloff, who grunts.

"Gol-damn, git the hell out b'fore I shoot yer pecker off!"

Carloff pulls his gun and stabs the barrel at the cowboy's groin. The itchy-fingered rustler jerks his hand from his britches, holds the liquor bottle close and staggers to the door.

"I ain't done nothin' wrong for ya to point yer gun at me."

"Share them crotch-crickets 'nd I'll shoot ya for sure!"

The cowboy stands at the door flushed with anger, but too drunk to do anything about it. He glances down to his pistol in the holster at his side then pushes through the crooked batwings and walks past the window. He briefly peeks inside at the game, looks down the street at several men by the livery barn, then steps around to the outhouse in back.

Arriving across the street from the saloon, the two lawmen stop and look the drinking establishment over. The Territory Marshal turns to Elkman and McGredy and addresses them firmly.

"This is a law matter. You both wait here on the boards while we handle this."

The deputy raises a muddy boot to the boardwalk and leans forward with his shotgun loose over his arm. He wipes the last of the sleep from his eyes and half-grins.

"Them boys are probably still havin' their breakfast. We'll jest amble in and bring 'em out with us."

McGredy shakes his head at Elkman who seems conflicted at the turn of events and plan of execution. The gambler angrily holds his rifle at the ready.

"We ain't even gonna get a shot at them?"

Elkman looks to the marshal and deputy then back at McGredy.

"The marshal is right. This is a law matter. We're not vigilantes and got no right to act that way."

"What about the kid?"

The marshal looks sternly toward McGredy.

"He'll get justice, not revenge."

McGredy's jaw clenches hard as he glares at the lawman.

"I don't think you understand. Those men ambushed us and killed one of ours. They're drinking in there, not havin' Sunday tea 'nd biscuits! They need to be dealt with accordingly."

With stony mature eyes, the marshal stares down McGredy.

"I said we'll handle it according to the law. If they are the fellers that stole your horses, they'll answer for it. I'll not have half-cocks and hotheads shooting up a town in my jurisdiction, no matter the poor reputation."

The marshal puts up a resolute hand and motions for them to stay on the boardwalk facing the saloon.

"We'll handle this peaceably."

The deputy pulls his hobble leg down off the boards and nods his bearded chin toward Elkman and McGredy. The two stand and wait, rifles in hand, watching the pair of aged lawmen advance toward the den of thieves.

The senior pair of peace officers passes the midway point in the muddy street and the marshal speaks quietly under his breath to the deputy. "Got 'em side by side 'nd six around?"

"Yup . . . loaded for b'ar."

The two seasoned lawmen continue on toward the saloon. The marshal stares at the card playing men through the lit glass panes of the saloon and steals a glimpse at his deputy.

"Easy on trigger but fleet of foot if it comes to shootin'."

Putting a hitch in one of his hobble steps, the deputy pulls back both the paired hammers of the shotgun and raises it to waist level.

Chapter 29

The wet mist in the air has faded with the morning light to leave remnants of a cloudy hue. East of town, cresting low over the hill, the sun rises to cast long shadows down the damp street. The two lawmen stop several feet from the front walk of the saloon and peer into the lighted window to see the players around the card table. There is a nearby creak and slam of a flimsy built door. The two law officers in the street snap to the ready as they turn their attention toward the outhouse next to the building.

A cowboy emerges from the latrine facilities with his pistol and gun-belt over his shoulder and a whiskey bottle tucked under one arm. He gazes downward, scratching and buttoning his britches, and grunts as he takes a step forward. The marshal quickly glances at his deputy and calls out. "Hold it . . ."

As the words of caution pass the lawman's lips, he pulls both pistols and eases the hammers cocked with a dual set of clicks. The cowboy stops fastening his button-fly and slowly looks up to scan the street in front of the saloon. He seems almost detached from reality and drunkenly unaware as he stares at the two old men with guns and law badges at the ready. His gaze travels across the street to Elkman and McGredy, and a spark of recognition shows in his eyes.

The rustler suddenly grabs for his pistol, drops the whiskey bottle, and snaps off a shot toward McGredy. The bullet skitters across the muddy street as McGredy raises his rifle and returns the exchange of lead. A second set of missed gunshots are swapped between the two before the marshal calls out.

"Hold yer fire!"

The rustler spins toward the lawman, fans the hammer on his Colt pistol and fires again, hitting the marshal in the leg and dropping him to the ground. The deputy instantly puts his scattergun to his shoulder and lets go with both barrels toward the outhouse. The broad spread of pellets hits the rustler around the upper chest, bloodying his shirt and face, tumbling him back against the outhouse door.

Guns ready, Elkman and McGredy step from the boardwalk and advance toward the saloon. Squatted in the muddy street, holding his leg, the marshal turns to Elkman and holds up his pistol broadside.

"Stay where you at! We'll handle this."

The deputy breaks open his double-barreled lead-slinger, dropping two empty brass shotgun shells to the street. He grabs two more from his coat stash and brings them to his whiskered lips to blow off the pocket lint. He slams them in with a hollow *thunk* and snaps the breach closed.

The injured rustler twitches against the wood slat outbuilding, drops his pistol to the ground, and slides down the door to slump in a pile. The batwing saloon entrance suddenly swings open and Boss Carloff and several others step outside. At the sight of the two lawmen in the street with the shotgun still smoking, the few bystanders scatter like roaches. Snarel peers over the shoulder of one of the rustlers and spots McGredy on the far boardwalk. He pulls his pistol and snaps off a shot.

The wood post near McGredy's head splinters with the bullet hit. McGredy fills with rage as he shoulders his rifle and fires toward the saloon. Snarel fires again over the shoulder of the nearby rustler and the man holds his ear from the ringing explosion.

As Elkman and McGredy advance into the street, levering their rifles, Boss Carloff and the other rustler pull their guns and enter the shooting fray. Caught in the crossfire, the two lawmen begin to scramble for shelter across the street from the saloon.

The deputy unloads his shotgun again on the front of the saloon to protect the wounded marshal's retreat. One load tears into the sign over the door and the other explodes the glass framed windows. The outlaws at the saloon entrance quickly dive for cover and duck back inside. They shoot from the doors and broken windows, throwing shots across the street while the two lawmen crawl to refuge behind a stack of mercantile crates.

Elkman moves to shield himself behind a horse watering trough and fires his rifle over the top. Several rounds plink into the wood around the door and through the window but miss their marks. He looks up at McGredy still standing and levering away like an invincible man. Elkman hollers at him over the gunfire.

"Get down, ya damn fool . . ."

Behind the trough, squatted on the ground, Elkman leans against the wooden water tank and reloads from cartridges on his belt. He fills the rifle's magazine tube and feels his hand around his ammo belt for an estimated count of reloads.

In the hail of gunfire, a bullet tears through McGredy's shoulder, spinning him to the ground. Elkman curses under his breath and sets his firearm aside. He quickly reaches out and snatches McGredy's rifle from the ground and grabs the burly man by the shoulder of his vest.

"C'mon, ya dunderhead, roll yer big ass o'er here."

McGredy gives Elkman a queer look as he digs in his boot heels and scoots behind the water trough.

"I'm shot... ya should be nicer to me."

"Ya got shot from standing around firing yer rifle like yer at a gol' damned carnival shootin' gallery!"

"I was covering you!"

"This water bucket was covering me jest fine!"

Elkman pushes McGredy's rifle to its owner and picks up his own.

"You hit bad?" Pulling his hand away, McGredy looks at his bloody shoulder.

"Looks as if it jest skinned me."

A bullet splashes water from the trough and Elkman leans his rifle over the top edge. Taking aim, he fires and levers another round into the chamber. He glances over as McGredy pops his head up to watch. McGredy draws his sidearm and fires several shots that go terribly astray. Elkman shakes his head, disgusted, and snaps off another shot.

"Keep yer head down."

McGredy smiles at Elkman, then ducks down holding his pistol across his wounded shoulder.

"Reload my rifle for me or I won't be able to hit any of 'em from here."

Elkman lays down his long-gun and snatches McGredy's rifle from the ground. With his elbow leaned in the mud, Elkman takes a handful of cartridges from McGredy's belt and starts to slide them into the side-gate.

"You couldn't hit any of 'em when you were shooting this thing before. Is yer barrel bent?"

Elkman slides the last cartridge into the brass receiver and eyes down the sights. McGredy holsters his pistol and winces at his shoulder pain.

"Definitely cain't hit 'em this distance with my pistol."

McGredy peeks around the water trough and looks over toward the lawmen behind the stack of crates.

"Them old tin-stars sure didn't help the situation much."

"They're the law hereabouts."

"Don't matter much now as they seem about shot to hell."

Elkman passes the rifle back to McGredy and the stout gambler levers a round into the chamber. He winces at the pain in his shoulder and positions himself to take aim.

Inside the saloon, the shooting stops momentarily and the three rustlers pull back from the windows and batwing doors to reload. Snarel eyes the back entrance and the stairs leading to the upper loft. He watches Carloff rotate the fastening buckle of his ammo-belt to the back and pull brass cartridges from the loops. Carloff ejects the spent casings, reloads, and mutters with trepidation.

"There's only three of us left."

"What of it?"

Carloff snaps the loading gate shut and looks to the rear entrance.

"Let's skedaddle out of here."

His demeanor turning dangerously dark, Snarel glares at Carloff.

"Ya damned coward! I already hit the big guy . . . only one of them out there yet.

"What the hell ya mean, only one of 'em?"

"Those broken-down lawmen ain't going anywhere."

"Yeah, that's the thing . . . we just gunned down the damned Territory Marshal. They'll string us up for that."

Snarel stares coldly at Carloff.

"You think horse rustling' ain't a hangin' affair? Jest need to make it so there ain't a soul to tell no tales."

Snarel cocks his revolver and turns to the other rustler at the window. He points the barrel at him and motions to the back door of the saloon.

"You . . . head out around back and see if you kin sneak up and shoot any of them bastards."

With a quick glance between Carloff and Snarel, the rustler looks down at his pistol. He steps away from the window opening, dumps several spent shells, and reloads from his belt. On his way to the back of the room, he grabs up a whiskey bottle and takes a long swallow before slipping out the back door.

Chapter 30

The brief silence in the hushed street hangs thickly with a black powder haze while both sides reload firearms and take stock. Elkman watches the Territory Marshal leaned up behind a crate holding his bleeding leg as the deputy kneels next to him with the shotgun perched over the top of a wooden box. Elkman slides a couple more loads into his rifle and looks to the few remaining cartridges in his belt. He turns to McGredy and talks low.

"If this don't end soon, we're gonna run out of lead to toss at each other. That lawman will bleed out and the deputy might just die from old age."

McGredy looks down at his mostly empty cartridge loops.

"They cain't be too well supplied in there either."

"Who knows, the barkeep could be the gunsmith in town. They may be able to hold out in there for weeks."

McGredy smiles at Elkman.

"Fine time for you to get a sense of humor . . ."

The barrel ends of two guns poke from the saloon door and the bark of flaming pistols resumes. McGredy ducks down as splinters of wood and water kick up from the horse trough.

"Their aim seems to be improvin' too."

"And they're just usin' sidearms."

"They got the advantage of bein' uphill from us and ain't crouched in a puddle behind the horse drink."

Elkman watches as one of the rustlers moves out from the back of the saloon and up the stairs to the building next door.

"Damn it! There one goes out the side."

The two watch, under a hail of gunfire from the saloon, as the rustler tops the stairs and ducks in one of the doors. McGredy snaps a shot off at him, missing by three feet and shattering a window. He levers his rifle again and looks toward Elkman.

"Go git him, I'll cover ya."

Elkman looks at McGredy like he's jesting.

"Yeah sure, dead-eye."

Seemingly hurt at the derogatory remark referencing his shooting, McGredy shrugs and points to his bleeding shoulder.

"You're not wounded . . ."

"I'd like it kept that way. You said it was just a scratch."

McGredy rolls his shoulder and winces.

"It might be more'n that."

Raising his head above the water trough, Elkman scans the street.

"Fine, I'll go. You better throw some lead."

"I'll git ya 'cross the street."

Elkman slides his pistol from the holster at his hip and sets his rifle aside. He opens the loading gate on the long barreled conversion revolver and keeps his head low behind the wooden water barrier. He spins the cylinder to make sure of his load, six around, and snaps the gate closed. Several shots whiz over their heads as Elkman looks to McGredy who grimaces reassuringly.

"Ready, McGredy?"

McGredy smiles and nods again.

"On yer move."

Inhaling a chest full of air, Elkman leaps out from behind the water trough and dashes into the street. He fires several times toward the saloon and once up toward the balcony on the building next door. McGredy pops up with rifle in hand and levers through the magazine, spraying bullets all across the front of the saloon.

Elkman ducks to cover under the upper porch on the building next to the saloon and looks back to see McGredy reloading the rifle with the last of the ammunition on his belt. He slowly moves around to the side of the building where stairs lead to the upper level. As he begins to climb the stairway, the rustler comes out and takes aim down on the street over the banister. Elkman raises his pistol and calls out.

"Put 'er down!"

The rustler quickly spins on his heels and snaps off a shot at Elkman that barely misses. Elkman presses himself back against the plank wall and fires his pistol. The bullet tears into the rustler's left arm, which turns him and causes a misfire of his second shot into the boards near his feet. Elkman cocks back the hammer and squeezes the trigger again only to hear a frustrating empty *click*.

Not wasting a moment to escape, Elkman grabs hold of the stair rail and leaps over to the ground as the rustler fires off several more shots at him. He rolls under the open wood-framed staircase and scrambles to reload. Hands deft and steady, Elkman ejects an empty brass casing and slides a loaded cartridge in. He spins the cylinder and looks up to the man coming down on him.

From above, the rustler fires two more shots that tear through the wooden stair treads. He takes another step down when a single rifle shot separates itself from the rest of the commotion. The rustler stumbles, then crumples, and falls against the wall.

Elkman crawls out from under the stairs and looks to McGredy who makes a flagrant gesture with his smoking rifle from across the street. Moving around to the base of the steps, Elkman raises his cocked firearm at the wounded man.

"Toss aside that Colt."

"I'll be damned if I'll hang . . ."

"You'll be damned either way."

The rustler squirms in pain with a rifle bullet through his shoulder and one in his left arm. He suddenly raises his pistol again and fires his last shot at Elkman, missing wide. In an unchecked reaction, Elkman jerks the trigger and the pistol's fiery discharge lodges in the man's chest cavity, stopping him dead. The rustler stares coldly ahead until his eyes go dark and he tumbles down the rest of the stairs to land at Elkman's feet.

The dead man heaped before him, Elkman opens his revolver and dumps the empty shell casings from the cylinder one by one. He reloads rounds from his belt as he turns and strides toward the saloon's back entrance. Gunfire can be heard continuing at the front of the building as he reaches the back door which sits slightly ajar.

Elkman eases the side gate of his pistol closed and holds it at the ready as he cautiously reaches out to the brass doorknob. The door gently pushes open from inside and the double barrel of a side by side scattergun pokes out. Flattening himself against the wall, Elkman watches as the apron-clad bartender creeps out the back entrance.

Elkman holds back and waits as the barkeep pokes his exposed head around the door. He looks down at the sawed-off shotgun, then at his own single-action pistol in hand. Removing his finger from the trigger, he swings the barrel down hard on the man's hatless head, splitting the thin balding skin over his skull. The bartender drops to the ground, rolls, and looks up in a daze.

With a backhanded swing, Elkman pistol whips the man across the temple which slumps him to the ground, unconscious. Elkman steps to the other side of the door and waits for any others to follow. After a long moment, he picks up the shotgun, uncocks the hammers, and tosses it away in the tall grass. Quietly, he steps over the unconscious barkeep at the doorway and in through the back entrance.

Chapter 31

Setting his empty rifle aside, McGredy grabs up Elkman's long gun and takes aim over the wooden trough. He looks up the street at the wounded marshal leaned over, nearly passed out, and the deputy by his side blasting away with his shotgun occasionally and ducking back. Firing another errant shot, McGredy pulls the rifle down and levers another round into the chamber. He shakes his head and looks grim.

"Things ain't lookin' up fer Law 'nd Order . . ."

Shots continue from inside the saloon. Bob Snarel and Boss Carloff take deliberate aim out the front door and window, sending chunks of splintered wood and water splaying over their intended target. Snarel pulls back inside and empties his spent cartridges. He dumps a box of ammo on the card table and begins to reload, clicking the cylinder slow and methodical.

"Carloff . . . How many reloads do we have in here?"

Carloff fires off another shot and looks to the saddlebags hanging over the back of a chair.

"Enough to last 'em out if they don't go for help."

"Help? Where the hell they gonna get help?"

"I dunno, I didn't even know there was any law in town."

Snarel snorts as he closes his pistol and moves back to the door. He takes aim at the deputy and waits for his head to peek out from hiding before he snaps off a shot. The deputy's hat flies back with a bullet across the brim and the old man ducks down, out of sight. Snarel laughs and gives his gun a fancy twirling spin on his finger.

"There won't be much law in this town again soon."

Carloff takes careful aim at McGredy and puts another bullet in the top of the water trough. He laughs as the water splashes up with the thud of the lead projectile.

"I ain't had this much fun plinkin' in days . . . at least since we stole them horses, eh?"

Carloff looks over and grins through his long mustache.

"The gambler fella is poppin' his head up like a gin-sozzled gopher. He jest keeps gettin' wetter and angrier! Ain't seen the other one in a long while . . . maybe I bounced one through 'em?"

Snarel moves over to the window near Carloff and peers out trying to get a better vantage on the shielding water trough.

"I don't see the other one either. You let him slip away?"

Carloff eases back to the table and reloads.

"Where can he go to? You think Jimmy got 'em?"

Snarel leans out farther, trying to see the building next door and pulls his head in quickly as a rifle shot smashes nearby.

"I don't see 'em over there."

"Well, he could be on the upper decking."

A hail of buckshot scatters across the front of the saloon and the two rustlers watch the window as shards of glass fall to the floor. Snarel throws another shot out toward the deputy and tries again to get a view of the adjacent two-story structure.

"Cain't see too well from here without gettin' peppered by that old stinker with the scattergun."

Snarel steps back to the doorway and stares at Carloff while he loads his pistol then returns to the window. They both resume firing until Snarel holds up his hand and steps back to listen in the quiet lull of gunfire.

"I don't hear nothing from over there, he could'a run off?"

"Naw, he wouldn't do that."

They both hold their cocked and loaded guns at the ready, listening to the occasional pop of gunfire coming from outside. Snarel takes another shot at McGredy, which seems to hit on target, laying the gambler out of view behind the trough.

"That town lawman is out and I think the big guy is down. We get that other cowboy and it'll be a clean sweep."

"What about the deputy?"

"That old shit-slinger is probably about out of shot-shells. Doubt he can use a pistol and he'll probably die from fright before we end this thing."

They both laugh, wickedly amused, and resume firing their guns out the doors and window.

Concealed down behind the water trough, McGredy lies, unmoving, as water splashes over him. He winces every time a bullet tears into the wood, sending wet splinters all around. He levers Elkman's rifle and sees the chamber empty.

"Best hurry it up, Tomas . . ."

Several more shots slam into the thick sides of the trough and slosh the water skyward. McGredy gives a big sigh as water drips off the brim of his hat down into his chin whiskers. He sets the Winchester rifle aside, reluctantly drawing his sidearm.

At the back of the saloon, Elkman moves up quietly behind the two occupied gunmen and holds out his pistol, taking aim. He slowly cocks his revolver and decides who to put a bead on first. Staring coldly at the two men responsible for killing young Kent, Elkman grits his teeth and glares.

A long moment passes as Snarel and Carloff continue to shoot their guns out the front. Elkman lowers his aim and blasts one of the glass bottles from the nearby table. The broken shards and whiskey spray over the two unsuspecting gunmen and they spin toward him in shocked disbelief. Elkman raises his aim and motions the tip of his gun barrel to the table with the shattered bottle.

"Put them shooters on the table!"

Boss Carloff lowers his gun and moves toward the table. He stops when Snarel puts out his hand and motions for him to stay put.

"Hold on there a minute…"

Snarel looks to Elkman with the gun pointed at him directly and smiles his wicked, corn-toothed grin.

"Good to see you again, *friend.*"

"Cain't say the same."

The air still hangs with gun-smoke as Snarel wipes a hand across his mouth and slowly cocks his pistol.

"You won't shoot. You owe me still, remember?"

Tilting his head, perplexed, Elkman stares at the shady character of Bob Snarel, with anger and confusion in his eyes.

"How you figure?"

"Ya don't remember leaving me to die out there?"

"Should have done one better."

Snarel looks over to Carloff and gives a slight nod while slowly raising his gun. Elkman's eyes dart to the pistol in Snarel's hand.

"Ya don't set that piece on the table right quick, I'll be sure to fix the oversight."

The two rustlers step forward to lay their pistols on the table and Snarel quickly aims at Elkman and pulls the trigger. The hammer falls with a loud *click.*

Startled, Elkman stands his ground and glares at Snarel with contempt. Using the distraction, Carloff seizes his opportunity and raises his revolver. Elkman quickly turns his aim and, with a primal survival instinct, blasts Carloff in the chest.

Pushed back against the wall, Carloff lets out a yelping grunt, drops his pistol, and falls through the batwing saloon doors. Elkman quickly aims his pistol back to Snarel, who eyes another loose firearm on the table. A deep guttural rage swells in Elkman as he hollers at Snarel.

"Damn you!"

The scraggy bandit smiles as he tosses his empty pistol to the floor and nods over his shoulder to where Carloff fell.

"You jest kilt that man. I didn't think you had it in you."

Elkman takes a short step toward Snarel near the door and lowers his pistol aim to waist level.

"Don't believe I need any more of an excuse to burn you down right here and now."

Snarel stares down to his discarded pistol near their feet and shrugs as he looks out the door.

"Kill me now and you'll hang yerself alongside me as a cold-blooded murderer. The law is jest outside waitin'. Ya should've done it already when you had the mind to."

"No one is here to tell different."

The bandit glances down at Elkman's pistol aimed near point-blank a short distance from his chest.

"I knew it was empty . . . ."

He turns away from Elkman and pushes open the batwing doors laughing over his shoulder.

" . . . but you didn't."

Elkman glares at Bob Snarel and struggles between his feelings of justice and revenge. Snarel looks back and grins.

"Say, how did that boy make out?"

Snarel laughs smugly and suddenly the butt of a rifle stock slams into his face. Following the cracking impact, Snarel reels back with a blood smattered and busted mouth. He falls over a chair and tumbles to the floor, squirming in pain.

McGredy steps through the still swinging doors with rifle held high across his chest and grimaces when the door bumps his wounded shoulder. He watches as Elkman drops his gaze to the gun in hand and slowly lowers the hammer on the revolver. McGredy looks again to Snarel writhing on the whiskey soaked plank floor among empty brass shell casings.

"He isn't worth it."

Elkman stands in bemusement as the adrenaline continues to pulse through his veins. He stares blankly at McGredy, steps back, and slumps into one of the barroom chairs. Letting his gaze fall to the floor, Elkman nods in silent agreement.

Chapter 32

The Territory Marshal of Twin Fork Gulch sits behind a broad wooden desk and looks up when he hears a knock at the door. He glances to the upright gun rack on the wall stacked with a rifle and two short barreled shotguns. Subtly, he slides open one of the upper desk drawers, revealing a pistol within easy grasp, and calls out to the announced visitor.

"Come on in."

The door opens with a slow drag across the floor. Elkman steps into the sparsely furnished office followed by a reluctant McGredy. The lawman touches his hand to his bandaged leg under the desk and ushers them in with a wave from the other.

"Pardon me for not standing. Step over and have a seat."

Elkman takes a chair from near the wall and sets it in front of the marshal's desk. Hesitant to enter further, McGredy looks around the office and to the small holding cell in the back.

Through the partially closed doorway he can see Bob Snarel with a busted mouth, sitting on a cot in the hand-forged iron cage staring back at him. They each watch the other with obvious contempt. The marshal notices McGredy still standing by the door and clears his throat.

"Mr. Smith . . . isn't it? Would you like to have a seat?"

McGredy takes a moment to recognize his alias and jostles the door shut behind him. He grabs up a chair by the back rest, scoots it to the desk, and sits awkwardly. Elkman turns and gives him a reproachful look for his odd behavior.

The marshal shuffles through some wanted posters on his desk and Elkman leans forward to get a glimpse at some of them.

"Yer deputy said you wanted to talk with us."

"Don't know if you're familiar with these fellers, but there's a cash bounty on 'em."

McGredy stops shifting in his seat and perks up.

"How much?"

The old lawman flips through the posters again, stopping at a sketch that looks vaguely familiar to McGredy. He looks up at the two men before him curiously.

"You ever been to Cedar City?"

McGredy squirms a bit and looks to Elkman.

"No, don't think so . . . why?"

Elkman gives a negative turn of his head and the marshal continues through the stack. He pulls three from the pile and tucks the rest in his drawer behind the pistol.

"Well, two of them fellers are worth a fair 'mount. The other don't pan out for much."

McGredy licks his upper lip and wipes his whiskers. "That's fine, we'll take it."

The marshal looks up to McGredy with a questioning eye. Elkman puts his hand to the desk and gives it a diverting tap.

"Excuse our haste, but this wasn't what we set out to do and warn't 'xactly on our path of travel. We've got our stock back and need to git movin' on gather'n the rest of our gear."

With his attention turned to Elkman, the marshal nods.

"I understand your situation and I appreciate what you've done, but the thing is, this is a temporary office. I can't pay out the bounty to you here. It has to be processed in Cheyenne before it can be paid out there."

McGredy shakes his head annoyed.

"Cheyenne?"

"It'll take a few weeks, but once it's processed I can have 'em send you the bounty wherever you're headed with that stock."

Elkman thinks a moment as McGredy grimaces. He gives the desktop another tap of his fingertips, looks to McGredy, and nods.

"That'd be fine. Have it sent post to Virginia City in Montana Territory, care of my name."

"What about you, Mr. Smith?"

McGredy looks around confused.

"What about me?"

"Where should I send your share?"

Sitting uneasy under the steady gaze of the marshal, the gambling man struggles to retain his poker face and squirms in his seat.

"Send'n it in his name will be jest fine."

Contemplating McGredy a long moment, the attentive lawman finally looks down and makes a few notes on each of the wanted sheets. Pushing back in his chair, he grabs a single crutch from against the wall and uses it to stand.

"Your money will be there in a few weeks."

The marshal limps around the desk while Elkman and McGredy stand. He extends his hand to them both and they move toward the office door. Looking back into the jail area, Elkman pauses. "What's the lot fer 'im?"

He looks past the cell door to see Snarel watching through the fragmented light from the barred window. The marshal follows Elkman's gaze and adjusts himself on his crutch as he looks back at the prisoner.

"In this territory, a man who uses a sticky rope chooses to be hanged from one."

A raspy cough is followed by a lump of saliva launched across the back room, splatting near the cell entryway. Bob Snarel stands, wipes his mouth whiskers slowly, and puts his hands to the bars on the jail cell.

"I ain't been killed yet!"

The marshal takes a hobbled step toward the offensive spittle and gives the nearby spittoon a whack with his crutch. The brass receptacle tumbles across the back room and clangs into the cell's iron slabs.

"Use this for what's intended or I'll have you hog-tied for the duration of yer stay."

McGredy stands outside the front entrance, ready to leave. Elkman hesitates, then steps toward the cell confinement area. He pushes the secondary jail door open with his boot and it swings slowly clear. Elkman stops at the bars, face-to-face with the bandit Bob Snarel, and their eyes lock in an intense gaze. The scraggly prisoner remains silent. Elkman speaks low and slow.

"That boy you kilt was nigh on twenty years old . . . he was just coming to experience life. Was a terrible misdeed you done."

Snarel glares at Elkman as they stand opposite sides of the flat hammered cell partition.

"It's a tough world out there for young'uns."

Elkman looks through the iron-banded window to the sky outside.

"Folks like you make a prison for yerself anywhere ya go."

"You've left me for dead b'fore. We'll see how it works out this time. I've slipped from the reaper's grasp more'n once."

Elkman studies the unrepentant man a moment then turns to leave.

"No one around to save yer hide this time."

He feels Bob Snarel's eyes bore into him as he walks past the marshal and gives a nod. The captive prisoner kicks his boot into the bars and rattles the cage.

"I'll outlive you sons-of-bitches yet!"

Grim-faced, Elkman follows McGredy outside without looking back. The wounded marshal leans on the outside of the building and speaks to the men standing on the boardwalk.

"I am sorry to hear about your young partner. That man will be judged and punished accordingly."

Elkman turns and scans the now quiet town. The street and cool air is now clear from the gunfight of the day prior.

"How's yer leg?"

"It'll heal."

"How about yer deputy?"

"He's resting awhile. The fight took a lot out of 'em."

Elkman notices McGredy do a roll of his eyes and snort. He touches a finger at the brim of his hat to the marshal and nods.

"Thank ye for yer help."

The marshal leans forward on the crutch and looks toward the livery barn.

"You headed north from here?"

"We'll follow our back-trail a ways . . . gather our stowed gear then continue on."

"Good luck with the rest of your journey."

The wounded lawman adjusts his crutch as Elkman turns and follows McGredy down the boardwalk. He watches until they walk into the livery at the end of the street and disappear in the broken shadows of the corralled barn.

The midday sun sits high as the two partners ride through the sparsely inhabited town of Twin Fork Gulch. Running loose herd, they usher their stock through town. They ride past the deputy, who waves from a storefront porch, then continue past the bullet-riddled saloon that now sits dark and vacant. The two riders move at an easy pace, departing town by the same path they entered the day before afoot.

McGredy looks over his shoulder, eyeing the neglect of the once booming ore town, and gives a sigh of relief.

"Mighty glad to get out of there again. That place sure has the smell of death. Felt like a rope was going to get around my neck too if I stayed any longer."

"I reckon you tend to git that sort of feeling if you stay anywheres too long."

McGredy snorts and gives a chuckle with a twinge of nerves.

"You know it."

Elkman nudges his saddle mount and ushers the grouping of horses in front of him on. He slaps his rawhide riata along the side of his leg and glances over his shoulder.

"I get that feelin' jest bein' there with ya."

The two crest the hill to the east and ride the trail away, leaving the old mining town in the distance behind.

Chapter 33

Elkman and McGredy travel along natural wildlife trails that cross mountains, shallow streams, and vibrant landscapes. The dry, rocky terrain of the past weeks turns to lush patches of grass that swirl and sway against the knees of the driven horses. Ever vigilant to their primitive surroundings, the two riders pass unmolested by the native inhabitants or nature.

Along toward afternoon, perched on a ridge overlooking a valley with a creek below, the two watch a small herd of buffalo grazing near the wetland. McGredy takes his hat from his head and redefines the folds as he shapes the worn felt in his hands.

"Last time I was up this way they was a dozen times over."

Elkman takes his fixings from his vest and lets the trailing horses' lead rope fall limply over his lap while he rolls a smoke. The unattended horses drop their heads to eat from the sweet, green pasture that surrounds them. Elkman strikes a matchstick against the top of his saddle horn and watches as it flares and settles into an even burn. He leans into the short flame and puffs the hand-rolled.

"I ain't seen any buffalo south since seventy."

"Yeah, they used to wash over this land like a great wave of furry hide, horn, 'nd meat."

"Mostly gone now."

"Yep."

The two stand their horses and watch the bulky animals below as they grunt and cavort. McGredy smooths his hair back, puts on his hat, and overlaps his hands on his saddle horn.

"They sure look to have a good time."

Elkman lets out a hint of a smile as he watches a bull calf hop around the others, then fall down.

"His behavior looks familiar don't it?"

"You talkin' me dancin' on the bar . . . or the kid?"

McGredy shoots Elkman a sly grin. They both sit quietly remembering on the hard journey past and their young, former trail partner. Elkman holds his hand-rolled between gloved fingers, gives it a tap, and finally speaks.

"N'er did git that kid to a town for your barroom frolic."

They both nod silently while Elkman inhales and blows out a puff of smoke. McGredy stares forward and speaks aside.

"Folks like you is mostly gone now too."

Elkman raises an eyebrow toward McGredy.

"How's that?"

"I mean wanderin' folks that are quick with a gun."

"I ain't that quick."

McGredy shrugs.

"Seen you in a few shootin' scrapes and you ain't dead."

Elkman finishes his smoke and looks out over the few surviving buffalo. He crumbles the ash and remaining tobacco between his fingers, brushes it against his close-fitting leather chaps, and lets it fall to the breeze. He looks over at McGredy and smirks.

"Surprises me you ain't been kilt yet."

McGredy smiles.

"I enjoy life too much to get planted. Besides, I'm quick when it counts . . . in leaving."

They exchange an amused nod and look to the open horizon. Both take up their stock ropes and continue in a northerly direction.

The two cowboys lead the horses along a trail on a tall ridge. Elkman and McGredy look out over a basin to a dispersed settlement in the distance. The stock follows along as they ride abreast and Elkman squints to make out the faraway structures.

"What town do ya suppose that is?"

"Not sure, but it ain't Bozeman City."

They continue riding, quietly watching the small grouping of buildings as the afternoon light fades. McGredy adjusts himself in the saddle and looks around with a hint of recollection. Elkman notices his suspicious manner then speaks.

"You been in this area before?"

"Not sure 'xactly. These wide, open spaces mostly look the same in the territory."

"We'll ride into town, git our bearings and a few supplies."

"Sounds good to me."

"Yaugh . . . always seems to."

McGredy gives an innocent shrug then glances over toward Elkman who stares him down. "What?"

"Kin you keep to yerself while we git a few things or do I need to make sure there ain't a good game goin' in town?"

McGredy instinctively pats his vest pocket for his supply of winnings and smirks.

"I suppose I could keep to myself awhile."

"Yeah?"

"You trust me, don't ya?"

Elkman looks off to the town with only a few wooden structure buildings and houses.

"If there are wanted posters out on you, I'm not sticking around for a hearing. I'll just send you funds for a lawyer when I git to Virginia City."

The color fades from McGredy's face and he mumbles quietly as he rides ahead. "I'll keep it low key."

The two maneuver down from the ridge and continue on toward the assemblage of a town.

At the edge of the gathering of civilization, Elkman and McGredy approach the livery stables. A tall, lean man with long moustaches steps out of the barn and watches them approach. He moves over to one of the corral fences and swings the gate open for them to trot the horses inside.

Elkman and McGredy remove the lead ropes from the trailed horse stock and drape it over their saddle mounts before riding over to the Livery owner. The man does a quick count of the animals with his squinted eyes and wipes his lip-whiskers aside when he looks up at the riders.

"Want me to throw some feed in there for ya?"

Elkman rides closest and nods.

"Yaugh, jest grass'll do, thank ye."

The livery man looks the unusual pair of horsemen over curiously.

"Help ya fellers with anythin' else?"

Elkman pats the dust from his overcoat and looks to McGredy who stares toward a possible saloon with his eager attentions. Looking down at the livery man, Elkman gestures over his shoulder, out of town, and pushes his hat back on his forehead.

"Well sir, we just crossed over them mountains and are looking to git our bearings and some supplies."

The livery owner leans on the fence rail and turns his studied gaze from Elkman to McGredy.

"Whereabouts ya from and where you looking to get?"

McGredy senses a hint of familiarity in the livery man's voice and dismounts to loosen his saddle cinch. He stands concealed behind his horse and peers over the animal's neck before speaking.

"Aways south of here . . . and a bit further north."

The two men study each other a moment but neither seems able to fully recognize the other. Elkman leans back on the saddle cantle and scratches his whiskered cheek.

"We're delivering these horses from Colorado up to Montana Territory."

The livery man gives an amused chuckle.

"You fellers ain't as far off as ye might think. This here . . . is Montana, near as much most folks about figure it."

Looking around, McGredy studies the terrain in the fading light of evening as he adjusts his coat.

"Was a tad colder last time."

"Been here 'fore have ya? It's late in the season yet but yer lucky yous didn't git snowed on comin' over."

McGredy nods and moves to obscure himself toward the rear of his horse. Elkman watches his trail partner's strange behavior, then removes his hat to scratch at his sweat-matted hair.

"Montana, huh?"

"Yep, ain't no marker comin' in. Now that yer here and ya ain't been scalped or froze, where was it 'xactly you was headed?"

Elkman pulls his hat on, adjusting it for comfort and looks around at the town, then down to the livery man.

"The name of the town is Cameron. Supposed to be jest to the south 'nd east of Virginia City."

"Well . . . that's just about two days' ride north of here if ya ain't gone astray. Not much there. Ya git up to William Ennis' place 'nd you went too far."

Elkman gives a curious look to McGredy hiding out behind his mount and then back to the livery owner. He leans down and gives his horse a pat.

"Have 'nough room in the stables to keep us fer the night?"

"Kin even do you one better and offer ya a warm meal. My place is just around the corner and my wife is fixin' it now. She ain't much of a cook, but she don't burn it 'nd she's creative with what little we got."

Elkman steps down from his horse and stands opposite the fence from the livery owner.

"Much obliged."

"Kin I tell my wife to 'xpect two more then?"

McGredy peeks over his horse's neck.

"Yes, thank ye."

The tall lean man gives a smile and begins to walk away. He turns and calls out before he rounds the corner of the barn.

"Git yer gear unpacked and I'll be right back to help settle them horses in with some feed."

The two listen to the departing sounds of boot steps on gravel and a door creaking open nearby. Elkman unsaddles while McGredy leans on the tall fence and looks things over. There is a soft murmur of voices from the thin-walled house next door and McGredy whistles as he looks toward what little of town exists.

"He sure is friendly, nice setup."

"Yep."

"I think I've been here 'fore. Seems a mite familiar."

McGredy smiles to himself and Elkman ceases from the task of un-saddling.

"Should we 'xpect a visit from the law?"

"Naw, don't remember anyone gettin' killed . . . or there being any law abouts."

Elkman shakes his head and continues to unpack. McGredy watches a moment and pats his vest.

"Don't suppose you want to drum up a game of cards or some enter-tainment after dinner?"

"Nope."

Sliding a finger into his lower vest pocket, McGredy nudges his few remaining coins.

"If'n you don't want to gamble, could ya lend me a few dollars to git me started? Seems like I'm a bit low."

"Nope."

"Maybe jest a bit of an advance on these horses or that reward mon-ey?"

"We ain't been paid on either."

"Well, aren't you a tough hand to work with."

Elkman glances behind him at McGredy and gives a hard look.

"We're a few days out from delivering these horses, so I'd appreciate you takin' it easy till then."

McGredy rubs his whiskers and sighs.

"Yeah, probably better that way. I seem to remember what it was about this town now."

He smiles mischievously as Elkman unenthusiastically pulls his sad-dle from his horse.

"Should I ask?"

"Naw, it would probably jest upset ya."

Chapter 34

The morning rays of sun come low over the horizon, shining through the sparkling dew on the tall grasses at the edge of town. Their strings of horse stock assembled, Elkman settles up with the livery owner while McGredy waits mounted. Elkman shakes the tall, lean man's hand and steps to his horse.

"Thank ye for yer hospitality."

"Kerful on the way up to Cameron. This here can still be bad Injun territory. They come up quick and quiet."

Elkman slips a foot in the stirrup and swings into the saddle. He turns to McGredy, who jokingly looks around, wide-eyed, in all directions.

"Which way we headed again?"

"Hell of a scout you are . . ."

The livery man turns and points his arm.

"Due north, two days."

He pushes the corral gate open and Elkman and McGredy nudge their horses out. They urge the animals to a trot and lead the stock out of town with the sun warming on their right shoulder.

With the small settlement behind in the distance, McGredy looks back and laughs nervously. He jogs his horse alongside Elkman and pats his mount on the rump.

"Well, we made it out of another one unscathed."

Elkman shoots McGredy a scolding glance.

"What do ya mean? Something happen?"

The troublesome gambler steals another glimpse over his shoulder, shakes his head and combs his fingers through his beard.

"Nope, just feels good to be clear of that place again. I remember now . . . the last visit, I had an angry husband nippin' at my heels."

"That happen to you often?"

McGredy gives an impish grin.

"This one was ready to have me barked for my efforts."

"He was ta' scalp ya like an Injun?"

McGredy cringes and points down toward his lap.

"He was wantin' to cut off somethin' else."

Elkman grimaces in disgust.

"Any place you ain't worn out yer welcome?"

"Sure, probably a few."

The saddle pals exchange a familiar gaze and McGredy smirks. "Jest ain't been there yet."

McGredy chortles and Elkman spurs on ahead.

The two cowboys sit the evening around a small campfire. Elkman stares quietly, the flickering fire-light playing on his face, while McGredy listens into the quiet of the star-filled sky. The howl of a wolf call fades in the distant hills and the horses stand, peaceful and easy.

McGredy pokes the fire, stirring the glowing embers and looks up at Elkman with inquisitive eyes.

"Something on yer mind?"

Elkman breaks his gaze from the fire.

"Mixed thoughts."

McGredy taps his stick on a burning branch and guides the broken piece back into the coals.

"Glad to be done with these horses?"

"Yaugh."

McGredy studies Elkman as his stare falls back to the fire.

"That all?"

With a slow shake of his head, Elkman looks away then decides to place another stick on the campfire. They both watch the flames slowly rise up and curl around the dry timber.

Elkman looks dismal as he grits his teeth and pushes his tongue around inside his mouth with thoughts of remorse and remembrances.

"Hate to be the ones to tell that feller 'bout his nephew being killed. It's something terrible to pass young, but to be murdered by a horse thief is a hard one to swallow."

"Puts a damper on goin' back to see his sister too, don't it?"

Elkman looks up at McGredy and shrugs.

"Probably not make it back that way anyway."

They sit quiet a moment and McGredy nods with understanding. He watches Elkman awhile then snorts with self-amusement.

"We're still in Injun territory. Ye may have ten arrows in ya and all the horses stole 'fore reaching that town of Cameron."

"Puts my mind to ease."

McGredy watches the flames lick around a glowing branch and slowly break in two. He looks to Elkman with the growing compassion of friendship.

"It warn't our faults we survived and he didn't. T'was his own choice to ride along north and this land ain't known for sparing the young and deservin'."

The two sit, remorseful for awhile. McGredy continues.

"It's a hard thing to tell someone his kin is dead, but that's just the way it goes out here. You're either the one standing over the mound or the one down in it."

Elkman stirs the small fire and nods without glancing up.

"Dyin's a part of life . . . ain't no way around it but it don't make it any easier on the livin'."

McGredy kicks his legs out and leans back on his pile of saddle gear. He grunts one of his throaty chuckles and laces his hands behind his head.

"Ain't nothing easy 'bout this life; believe me I've tried."

The mood lightens a bit. Elkman looks up at McGredy and silently appreciates their mutual bond of camaraderie.

"You kin be a good saddle pal sometimes, McGredy . . . when you ain't molestin' the cards and hobble yer tongue some."

The burly gambler sits across the fire from the abiding cowboy and scratches his chin whiskers.

"Well, hell, 'bout time you noticed."

Elkman grabs up a poker stick and looks to the fire.

"You finished with it?"

"Yep."

McGredy watches and pulls up his blanket around his shoulders as Elkman scratches out the flames. A slight smoke rises from the dull glow of embers and the star-filled sky illuminates the two men as they settle in, tucked under their coverings. The contented snuffle of the nearby horses settles peacefully into the coming chill of night and everything falls quiet.

Chapter 35

The serene break of day comes upon the countryside surrounding the small grouping of horses and the cowboy camp. Elkman and McGredy gather their gear and assemble the saddle panniers for the pack animal. The herd grazes idly as McGredy shakes out his sleeping blanket and rolls it against his knee. Elkman squats to fill his drinking cup with the last remains of the morning's coffee and scans the skyline. He sips from the lip of the steaming vessel and suddenly his body tenses, eyes fixed on the far horizon.

"McGredy, you spoke of Injuns last night. Which type are they in these parts?"

The gambler stops what he's doing, looks to Elkman then up to the hills following his partner's gaze.

"How do you mean?"

"The friendly kind, or t'other?"

McGredy sees the three silhouetted Indians on horseback near the crest of the distant hill.

"Both. We shouldn't stick around to find out though."

Elkman empties his remaining coffee over the dying embers.

"My feelings exactly."

Shaking his cup out, Elkman tucks it in his saddle bag and resumes packing.

McGredy grabs up his saddle and blanket and throws them over his mount. He watches Elkman as he walks his horse over to be saddled.

"We should hurry up and git I reckon."

"Where to, Mister Indian Scout?"

McGredy looks around and touches his pistol instinctively.

"What do you suggest?"

Elkman tosses his saddle over his horse and quickly but efficiently secures the cinch.

"Well . . . we can jest continue on as if we don't see 'em 'nd hope fer the best."

Looking at Elkman skeptically, McGredy slides his rifle into the saddle scabbard and makes sure it is seated proper.

"But, I can see 'em!"

Elkman slips his bridle over the horse's nose and pulls it up past the ears and forelock. Feeling the faraway inquisitive eyes upon him, he lets the reins fall to the ground. He sneaks a glance at the natives on the hillside then moves to the horse stock and starts to string them together.

"They're probably only after the animals and are weighing their options. If they thought they had the advantage, they would have took it already."

"You mean we're gonna do nothing but wait?"

"We're gonna trail toward Cameron on the double quick."

"Hell, that's a full day ride yet."

"What are the options? You're the one with all the experience with inquisitive natives."

McGredy holds one string of horses as Elkman assembles the next.

"Well Tomas, it's a bit different tale when you have the United States Cavalry riding behind you. Them hostiles can be a tricky bunch. What if they attack . . . better yet, what if there are more of 'em ahead waiting for us?"

Elkman walks his horse string to his waiting mount and steps into the saddle.

"If that happens, we best be quick 'bout doin' somethin'."

With a sour expression, McGredy climbs into the saddle and stares back at the three watching horseback figures defined by the morning sky.

"I don't like this plan a t'all."

Elkman prods his horse on and gives a tug to the lead rope while riding in a northerly direction. He looks back over his shoulder, first to the attentive natives on the hill, then to the fretful gambler watching the horizon.

"They ain't done nothin' as of yet. You got some time to work up a better scenario 'nd let me know how it'll play out."

McGredy wheels his horse around and leads his string of animals. He lopes alongside Elkman and glances back again.

"Ya don't suppose they'll give a friendly wave, satisfied with ticklin' the sky, and let us be on our way?"

"Not likely."

"But, it's possible?"

"Yaugh . . . but not likely."

Elkman and McGredy travel horseback along past the middle of day. They continue north while McGredy casually watches their back trail. The gambler studies the forms of the three distant natives as they shadow their path from afar and shakes his head, calculating the odds. Elkman continues riding without looking back. His eyes forward, he speaks aside to McGredy.

"They still there?"

"Yup . . . all three of 'em."

Elkman nods.

"That's good."

"How you figure that's good?"

"We know where they all are."

McGredy looks over his shoulder again, thinking and watching.

"Ain't you curious?"

"What about?"

"I ain't seen you look back once since this mornin'."

Eyes turned toward his trail partner, Elkman lets go a knowing smile and touches the brim of his hat.

"Haven't needed to. You been havin' yer head on a swivel 'nd keepin' a pretty tight watch."

"A good thing too since we're trailing all this four-legged temptation. We're jest a prize ripe fer the pickin'."

McGredy tugs at the lead rope and steals another short glimpse.

"Maybe we should run 'em awhile and see if we can lose their interest?"

"Better to save the horses for when we need 'em. They're gonna follow till they ain't gonna follow no more."

"Yeah . . . still don't like that plan of yours."

The two continue at a steady pace, a fast walk rather than a trot. Again, McGredy can't help but look over his shoulder to their native hangers-on. He scans the horizon slowly at first, then more anxious.

"Damn!"

"What?"

"They're gone."

Elkman turns in the saddle and looks to the surrounding terrain.

"That's not good."

"Now what?"

Elkman sucks in his cheek and runs his hand across his lip whiskers. He thinks as he studies the open terrain ahead.

"If we ride hard, we should make the settlement of Cameron by dark. If'n we don't pass it by."

McGredy turns to Elkman with a serious intensity.

"That's a big *if* out here."

Both look toward the vast vacant lands to the north. Elkman holds the reins in one hand and the lead string in the other while regarding their situation, unsure. He looks to the gambler and shrugs. "Maybe they turned back?"

"Yeah, to gather all their family and friends in the tribe. They don't 'xactly welcome what they figure as trespassers in these parts. I think our chances are better not missing Cameron."

Elkman scans the horizon one more time.

"Agreed."

"Let's git . . ."

The horseback riders' anxiety transmits to their animals as a nervous tinge of energy. McGredy holds back his fidgety mount as the trailing string crowds forward. He watches Elkman's horse hold its head high with nostrils flared. Elkman glances over his shoulder one more time and slaps his gloved hand against the flank of his anxious steed.

"Yeah, let's git!"

McGredy lets his horse rein free and tear off with nary a kick. Elkman gives the excited horse his head and urges him to stretch out into a gallop with the running herd in tow. With nothing but the gentle sway of nature all around, the two race across hilly open grasslands into the unknown ahead.

Chapter 36

The heavy panting and sharp breaths of running horses pounds across the landscape. Elkman and McGredy ease to an easy pace astride their winded mounts and slowly halt the procession of eager animals. The saddle horses glisten with sweat and white cakes of lathered foam linger near the cinch and saddle blankets. The riders remain watchful of their surroundings and tense in anticipation of a hostile encounter. Elkman's eyes dart across the landscape and he waits for McGredy to ride up alongside. The terrain is clear and Elkman takes a calmed breath.

"McGredy, with your vast experience in the ways of the north country inhabitants, what sorts of natives do you suppose were following us?"

The former military scout looks to Elkman, raising an eyebrow at his sarcastic tone.

"Sioux. Maybe Flathead or Cheyenne. Don't really matter if they're out for sport 'nd plunder. They was pretty far, couldn't git a real good look at their beading or arrow feathers."

"Hope to keep it that way."

"In my *vast* experience, I find that's the best method."

Elkman cracks a smile.

"How close do ya think we are?"

"To them Indians or the settlement?"

"Hopin' we're closer to the town than a raiding party."

McGredy stands in his stirrups and tries to look over the next rise.

"We should be gettin' near."

"Keep yer eyes open for any type of lights, cook-fire smoke, or other sign to keep us on course."

McGredy lowers himself back to the saddle and looks behind.

"Hope to spot something 'fore dark."

Elkman exchanges an unsure glance with McGredy and pulls his hat down farther on his forehead. The two push their horses on to a canter over rolling grassy hills.

The later part of day settles into evening as Elkman and McGredy continue to travel north. The two walk their horses beside one another and peer into the approaching darkness. They crest the top of a small hill and look around for any signs of friendly civilization. McGredy points to a faint spot of flickering light far to the north.

"There it is!"

Elkman studies the glimmering lights with a sigh of relief. He squints and strains his eyes to another far away point nearby.

"Damn . . ."

"What's the matter?"

Elkman extends his arm and points further to the east.

"There's another one."

The two ride ahead with the darkening edges of the horizon setting in all around them. McGredy groans as he points to another dim group of lights below the evening sky out west.

"One over here too."

Elkman observes each clustered grouping of lights, feeling disheartened at the prospective trap. McGredy mumbles to himself. "Looks like we've stumbled into a metropolis."

Curious, Elkman turns to McGredy.

"A what?"

McGredy gives a shrug and looks around.

"Which way? One of 'em has to be the town of Cameron."

"You'd think, wouldn't you?"

"Hell, I told you they were crafty. If'n we stay here, they'll git us in the night. Choose wrong 'nd we ride right to 'em."

As the horses walk into the dusk of evening light, Elkman studies the possible destinations. He touches his vest pocket containing his tobacco pouch.

"Suppose I have time for a smoke?"

"You figure'n it to be yer last?"

"Possibly."

"Only if ya got one for me too?"

Elkman taps his vest pocket and thinks aloud.

"With all the Indian activity about, I wouldn't be surprised if the burg stayed dark at night to keep from trouble. All we know is we're headed north and the town is in that direction."

McGredy turns to Elkman with a troubled expression.

"Don't say that . . ."

"On the other hand, the town's location ain't no secret to anyone but us, so lights is the best for keepin' away undesirables.

"Anything is possible out here in the territory. That's why I like to keep close to civilization where the gals are friendly and the nights don't sleep."

Elkman pulls his pistol and slowly spins the cylinder. He eases a cartridge from one of his belt's bullet loops and slides it into the chamber, loading it six around. McGredy watches him as he contemplates their options.

"What're you doing? You got a plan?"

Elkman holsters the pistol and pulls his rifle from the saddle scabbard. He chambers a round, eases the hammer down gently, and slides it back in the leather sleeve. He looks to McGredy and gathers a fist full of reins.

"I'm going on."

"Which way?"

Elkman nods forward and tugs his hat brim down. He looks to McGredy as he hunkers down in the saddle, ready to sink spur and make a run for it.

"Yer free to choose yer own direction or stay put. I won't hold it 'gainst you."

Elkman eases the horses into a faster pace and McGredy kicks his heels to keep up.

"Damn, Tomas, that's a fine thing to say after all we've been through together!"

As they lope along, McGredy pulls his pistol and holds it at the ready. He keeps the pistol in hand and loosely grips the lead rope to the trailing horse stock.

"What if the lights you choose is the wrong one?"

"You mean the one *we* choose?"

"Yeah . . . what if *we* ride into a dozen painted braves with their bowstrings stretched?"

They look to each other in the fading light and Elkman's eyes flash with roguish daring and resignation to their dire situation.

"We throw hot lead and get the hell out quick."

McGredy gives a nervous laugh and lopes his horse alongside his trail partner. He holds his pistol close and sits tight in the saddle.

"Has been good knowin' ya, Tomas H. Elkman . . ."

Chapter 37

The rising moon shines brightly on the treeless landscape. The two horse-back riders glide through the spreading nightfall, trailed by a flowing form of ghost-like animals that canter along with a steady cadence. Still a mile away, they approach the middle cluster of lights and Elkman tilts his head listening into the night. He slows his mount and strains himself to hear the looming sounds from the dark scenery.

"Hear that?"

McGredy lopes along, keeping snug in the saddle with an easy grip on the lead rope for his string of following animals.

"All I hear is my chest beat 'nd horses blow . . . what is it?"

A prolonged whistle through the air is followed by a solid *thud* and one of the horses screams agony into the throbbing silence of darkness. The shrill cry of the injured mare sends a tense shiver through the air. Elkman and McGredy hunker low on their mounts as arrows begin to whiz by around them. An arrow skitters off Elkman's leather saddle skirt-ing and he sinks spur as he tosses the lead rope aside.

"Let loose those horses 'nd head for the lights!"

In a flash, Elkman draws his stag-handled blade and cuts the injured horse free from the line-up. The remaining horses dash off in a tight cluster of flurried mane and tail. McGredy directs his pistol behind and snaps off a shot that nearly blinds the two riders in the blackness. He reins alongside Elkman as they move out quick from the occasional loosed arrow.

The two race across the terrain toward the faraway cluster of lights. Glancing over their shoulders at the Indian pursuers, the horseback forms are like devilish shadows charging against the moonlit sky. McGredy reaches back and fires off another shot that whirls into the following crowd and raises the whoop and holler of the natives. He turns to Elkman as they race along, side by side.

"How'd you know we're headed right?"

"I don't . . ."

Elkman and McGredy push their horses hard and feel the churned up and tiring muscles under them. They continue to gallop along, following their tangled grouping of fleeing horseflesh. Elkman winces as another arrow skims past his hand. He jerks his pistol and fires at a hostile rider coming up on his flank. The rider tumbles from his mount and is overrun by the following mass of howling pursuers.

Elkman watches ahead and notices their unburdened horse stock moving at a quicker stride toward the lights and hollers to McGredy.

"Hoping those horses lead us right!"

"I jest want to git somewheres quick…"

McGredy ducks lower at the relentless whistle of arrows and the occasional whooping war cry which seems to narrow in distance. They gallop over an earthen berm and the two cowboys make out the outlines of a few wood-framed structures and the elements of a town. With renewed vigor, they prod their chugging horses on, urging the heaving bodies of the animals beneath.

Elkman fires his conversion pistol behind him again several times, leaving the last round in reserve. With his horse stretched out under him at a fast gallop, Elkman jabs his sidearm in his holster belt and jerks his rifle from the scabbard.

"Bark that hogleg, McGredy! Let 'em know we're coming in hot!"

Arm extended back, McGredy sends off a shot without sentiment, then hammers two more in quick succession. He looks toward the approaching town and gives up a loud whooping holler. An arrow rips under his arm, slashing through his coat, and his eyes go wide as he hunkers down for the final stretch of the race to town.

In quick pursuit of their crazed herd of horses, Elkman and McGredy tear into town, kicking up a spectral cloud of dust. Backed by a two-story framed structure, Elkman leaps from his animal with his long-gun and shields himself behind the frothy saddle mount. Elkman pulls his horse's head around and props the rifle over the saddle-seat. He snaps off a shot and one of the pursuers tumbles from his war pony at the farther reaches of the building's lamplight.

McGredy levers and fires his rifle topside in the saddle and his horse shies from the gunshots with a bucking crow-hop. He ungracefully dismounts, stumbling to the ground, as his horse runs off down the street to the other loosely assembled stock. A half-dressed man in unfastened britches held up by galluses over long-underwear appears at the door behind them and calls out.

"What is this? What's the shooting about?"

He grabs a shotgun from inside and steps out as an arrow thumps into the boardwalk near his bare feet. Elkman continues to fire his rifle and McGredy ducks behind the hitching post yelling the alarm.

"Indians! Take cover!"

The man with the shotgun jumps back into the doorway and blasts off one of the barrels into the night and nowhere in particular.

"Get down there, fella . . ."

Elkman ducks down as the second shotgun blast seems to go just over his head. He peers under the belly of his horse at the hostiles near the far reaches of town and yells back to the storekeeper.

"Watch that scattergun!"

Elkman slaps the rump of his horse sending it further into town and steps away with his rifle behind a stack of burlap-covered supplies near the boardwalk. He looks over at McGredy's large frame behind the post of the hitch rail, then at the barefoot man in the doorway. He scans his rifle along the edge of darkness as the shooting stops and the smell of burnt gunpowder drifts through the cool nighttime air.

The scantly lamplit town is nearly silent as a wave of kicked-up, departing dust rolls through and settles. Several people awakened from the yelling and gunshots begin to emerge from the buildings, stepping out into the street.

"What's going on?"

McGredy stands and struts out from behind the hitching post. He dusts himself off and calls out to the growing crowd.

"All is well now, people, . . . the feathered bonnet natives 'round here jest took an interest to our travels."

A portly man with an old muzzle loader rifle moves across the street and addresses McGredy.

"Yer unlucky to be traveling at night. Folks don't usually leave the confines of town after dark on account of marauders. Where was it you were aiming for?"

Elkman steps over and adjusts his hat.

"Is this here the town of Cameron?"

The portly man scratches his exposed underbelly and peers at the two cowboys strangely. He eyes Elkman and nods.

"It surely is."

Elkman exchanges a look with McGredy who grunts satisfied.

"Guess we chose correct."

The town man guffaws.

"Ain't much of a choice to it. There ain't another hint of a settlement fer days 'round."

Elkman and McGredy both gaze out past the boundary edge of the buildings as the light from the town fades to blackness. The buckskin and feather clad form that fell moments before is gone and the quiet sounds of evening are all that remain.

Chapter 38

Morning breaks peacefully on the small, rural town in southwestern Montana. The wide, dirt street that bedded down with the evening's gunfire and native cry is now quiet, with only the cluck of chickens that pace and peck at the ground frost. At the end of town, the only goings-on are the stable corrals newly filled with horseflesh being fed. A thin waif of smoke settles across the street as the morning cook-stoves are warmed with fire.

Smells of breakfast emanate from a single, level wood-framed structure backed by a canvas grub shack. At one of the four tables inside, Elkman and McGredy sit and wait, listening to the rolling groans of their hungry insides. The smell of bacon and biscuits being prepared spreads across the room, intensifying their appetite. Elkman rests his bandaged hand on the table and glances around. The trail-worn pair seems rough and out of place in the simple, clean-swept room with linen tablecloths.

McGredy looks over his shoulder to the back service entrance and scratches his unshaven cheeks.

"Let's put this meal on the horse trader's account. I think I could eat a dozen or two eggs."

Elkman leans back in his chair and smiles.

"There are seldom times I'm in agreement with you, but this happens to be one."

They both glance over as the bar girl bumps her way through the partial door using her backside with two heaping plates of fare in hand. She sashays over to the table in a teasing way, cherishing the gut-wrenched hunger of the famished cowboys.

"Here you boys go. From the looks of it ya haven't had a horse from under ya, a roof over ya, or a good meal in a while."

McGredy nearly drools at the smells coming off the plate. He eyes the pork, eggs, bread, and steak as it sizzles on the tin plate.

"A grown man needs to eat like this every day. He cain't get nourished doin' himself on hard tack 'nd jerky."

The bar gal slides the hot plate in front of McGredy, tosses the hot-holder towel over her shoulder, and beams a slightly crooked-toothed smile. Her hard-used years seem to melt away with the affectionate attentions from McGredy. She sets the other plate of food before Elkman and smooths her hair back from her face. She twists the towel in her fingers while smiling down at them and lingers for compliments as they take up their eating tools.

Elkman lets the first hot mouthful slide down to his empty insides, and chews. He wipes his mustache and nods.

"Fine cooking, ma'am."

McGredy sits erect with his next forkful hanging in midair as he chomps. He gives her a lustful wink.

"I'd like to dive into this 'nd enjoy its flavors all day. It takes quite the woman to fix together vittles such as these."

With a twitter, the bar gal shakes her head at McGredy and slips her hands under her apron.

"I do like to see a hungry man eat. Somethin' about it makes my insides tingle."

Elkman takes another bite and peers up, amused at the flirty waitress and the philandering gambler seated across from him. The high-roller puffs out his chest and takes another mouthful.

"Well ma'am, I'm so hungry I could surely make you tingle all over."

She puts her hand on his shoulder and smiles warmly.

"I bet you could."

The barmaid turns back to the kitchen and peeks over her shoulder demurely, wiggling her rear-end.

"If'n you two need anything else you haven't had in a while, jest let me know."

McGredy grins at Elkman and nods, touching his hat brim toward the waitress woman.

"Thank you, ma'am. I'll mull on it over my breakfast."

She saunters away, revealing her strangely attractive jack-toothed smile, and wags a finger at them both. Elkman stops chewing a moment and stirs the beans and egg yolk on his plate with a wedge of thick-cut bread. He looks up and smiles at McGredy good-humoredly.

"It's been a long spell on the trail."

"She may not look like much, but she's got personality and a mite nicer to put my gaze upon than you and them horses."

"I'd rather not have thoughts of you 'nd her dancin' in my head while I eat."

McGredy shrugs as he shovels more food in his mouth.

"I don't mind seconds."

"You're a man with appetites."

McGredy wipes food bits from his chin whiskers with his palm holding the pronged eating tool and drolly looks to the cloth napkin in his other hand. He pauses, smiles at Elkman, and dabs his mouth daintily in a feigned act of polite manners. With his cheeks full and chewing, McGredy leans in to the table and talks through his swallowing gulps.

"How we gonna find this feller to git them horses to?"

Elkman stirs his plate and loads his utensil. He finishes his prior mouthful before responding.

"I put a word in at the livery and the hardware supply. They say today or the morrow, that feller should come get his weekly stores in town."

Raking his table tools across his metal plate, McGredy scrapes the remaining bits of food.

"I don't mind spendin' time here for a day or two . . ."

He glances back toward the grub-shack entrance.

". . . but them lonely gals do seem to get attached easily."

"We'll rest ourselves and the stock 'nd can figure for delivery on the morrow."

"Jest 'nough time to leave a good impression."

"Should've figured your style at the card table was about that speed under the quilts."

McGredy finishes his plate and licks his eating utensil.

"You stick 'round anywhere too long 'nd yer not welcome. At the game table 'nd with love, best to leave when you're ahead."

The light mood is broken by a man's shadow crossing the forward-facing window and the front door opening. Backlit in the entryway, a tall, lean western figure steps into the saloon and walks to the bar. He waits awhile for the male barkeep to come from the back and leans down on the bar-top to speak.

McGredy eyes the large Walker pistol hung on the man's hip and slowly puts his hand to his own firearm under the table. The gambler weighs the odds for trouble and steals a glance at Elkman while the newcomer talks in low tones to the barman. They both watch as the keeper behind the bar nods in their direction.

Striding over to the table, the unknown man looks vaguely familiar. Elkman and McGredy stare agape at the tall westerner as if confronted by a familial ghost. With a greying mustache hanging from his top lip, the eyes and features of the man look to be young Kent with several decades upon him. He stares down at the seated trail-hands and lets his probing eyes wander between the two as he stands over them.

"Excuse me . . . I'd like to introduce myself. I'm James Mitchell from over at the Lazy M bar ranch . . . I believe you're the fellers come into town with a delivery of horse flesh in tow."

Elkman slowly stands and puts out his hand.

"Yes, sir . . . the name's Tomas H. Elkman. This here is Jefferson McGredy."

James takes a firm grip to Elkman's hand, pumps it twice, and extends his hand down to the seated gambler.

"Been a hard trip for ya?"

McGredy tries to quietly un-cock the pistol laid across his lap. "How could ya tell?"

"Received a message from my brother a few weeks ago. Been expecting you or news of ya since."

James gestures toward the exposed pistol as McGredy tries to covertly holster it.

"Didn't figure you always put out to introduce yerself by drawing iron first."

McGredy half stands and shakes James's hand.

"Just a mite touchy yet. We run into trouble some."

"I heard how you boys came in hot-footed after dark last night. How many horses made the journey?"

Elkman eases back into his chair and looks away reverent, then down at his nearly finished breakfast. "All but one."

James nods and scans around the empty room.

"Where's Kent hiding? This was a helluva trip for 'em?"

McGredy places his hands solemnly on the table and lets his gaze fall to the floor. He gives an uncomfortable cough and avoids eye contact around the table. Elkman rises a bit in his chair and motions to an empty seat at the table.

"You best sit down."

James pulls back the chair, steps around it, and sits. He surveys the empty room again and looks to the back entrance.

"What happened? He git hurt?"

The silence in the room hangs with almost unbearable trepidation as Elkman removes his hat and grips it before him. He looks to the table, then up to McGredy before he scoots his chair back and speaks to the deceased youth's uncle.

"Young Kent there was killed by horse rustlers back in the Wyoming territory." James's face pales with the dreadful news while Elkman continues. "We buried him with a marker at a waterway near where it happened . . . the marshal in Henson County helped us recover the stock."

A vacant expression covers the mournful man's features and his eyes seem to take on a lonesome weariness at the loss. He takes a moment then looks up at Elkman.

"What about the men who done it?"

Elkman looks to McGredy who remains hushed.

"They paid for the misdeeds with their lives. Some of 'em fell to shootin' and t'others are to be put to the rope."

Elkman places his bandaged hand on the table and steals a glance over at the young boy's uncle. The stoic rancher lowers his head and a hint of tears twitch in his eyes as they glisten over in sorrowful longing.

Chapter 39

A new day dawns with a wide, blue, cloudless sky hanging over the empty streets of Cameron, Montana. At the edge of town, the occasional nicker from an isolated stud horse mixes with the sounds of the breeding stock being gathered. McGredy hangs lazily on a high-railed wood fence, watching as the others do the work from horseback.

With the strings of horses assembled and in tow, Elkman and the rancher, James Mitchell, ride out of the corrals and lead the stock into the vacant street. McGredy, looking cleaned up and washed, hooks his polished boot heel back on the rail fence. He puffs on a new clay tobacco pipe clenched in his teeth. Elkman looks down at him from horseback with an enquiring demeanor.

"Sure ya don't want to come along out to the ranch?"

McGredy lets out a puff of smoke and smiles up at Elkman who is freshly barbered and bathed but still retains his worn trail clothes. McGredy motions a grand gesture at his freshly laundered clothing using his pipe stem as a pointer.

"Once I get paid, my aspirations for work fade real fast."

He brushes off a smudge of dirt from his repaired jacket and sucks on the clay pipe.

"I'll meet you in Virginia City in a week or two. There is a certain activity I would like to attend to here 'fore heading out for the other."

Elkman shakes his head, smiling, as he glances to the cafe where they had taken meals the day prior.

"Don't let them new earnin's go burnin' a hole in yer pocket or git ya into too much trouble."

McGredy lets out another puff of smoke and laughs.

"Hell, you know me."

"Yeah . . ."

James patiently waits horseback as the two trail hands say their farewells. McGredy steps over and leans on Elkman's horse with his pipe-holding hand.

"Don't be puttin' any roots down b'fore I see ya again in Virginia City. You come there direct after you git them horses to their new spread 'nd I'll show ya a good time."

"Yup."

McGredy looks to James and tips a finger against the brim of his hat.

"Sir, it has been a pleasure."

"Yer efforts are much appreciated, Mister McGredy."

McGredy gives Elkman's horse a nudge on the shoulder as the two cowboys turn and lead the grouping of horse stock through town to the north. Midway down the main thoroughfare, Elkman turns back and watches as McGredy stands in the center of the empty street and throws a saluting wave. The lone gambler stands, silhouetted with his pipe clenched between his teeth and a waft of drifting smoke rising skyward.

The trail out to the Mitchell Ranch is more of the unaffected rolling, grass-covered range. Elkman leads his horse string near James and they ride along with a natural silence between them. The older man occasionally looks back at the trailing animals and carries the hang-dog look of loss, thinking on his deceased nephew. Elkman keeps his words to himself in his way that comes most natural.

After most of a day's ride, they crest a rim and look down toward a ranch setup reminiscent of the other Mitchell brother's spread farther south. James turns to Elkman and nods knowingly.

"I helped Henry build that house down yonder. Guess my carpentry skills are limited in vision."

"It's a good setup for a home no matter where you put it."

James holds back the horses and scans the spread. Down below, two men work behind a wagon filled with split wood poles. They fasten the length of rails between the uprights stuck in the ground, constructing more corrals. Elkman glances over at the rancher and the forlorn man wipes the moisture glistening from one eye. James sniffs slightly and stares across the valley below.

"I've been having them build a corral fence on and off for two years now."

James grits his jaw and continues.

"When I heard young Kent was comin' with the last group of stock I knew it would get through one way or t'other."

Elkman nods and speaks quiet and respectful.

"He warn't the young kid you probably last saw him as. He was a good hand and a fine young man."

James sighs and smiles.

"Yeah, and he probably had the stubbornness of his father and I when we were of that age."

"Yaugh, he did have a bit of that."

"He had his mother's fair looks."

"I warn't acquainted with her."

"Naw, she's out east somewheres."

Elkman feels pangs of longing as he thinks on his time spent with Kent's sister, Amy. He looks to the uncle and nods casually.

"I did not have the pleasure."

Removing his hat, James wipes back his graying mop of hair and takes a deep breath.

"There is a beauty to this country, but it is hard won."

He glances at Elkman to see if he is sounding tiresome and continues. "I had me a wife up here for a time. The long cold winters are hard on most but especially womenfolk. She kind of lost her way in the head."

James puts his hat back on his head and stares blankly off into the distance.

"I was out trying to keep what stock I had left gathered to survive in the cold . . . I come home to find her sitting out by the well pump, frozen stiff as a board . . ."

He shakes his head remorsefully, unloading a burden of guilt that has set down deep inside for years.

"The cabin was warm as toast . . . didn't have 'nough sense left to git out of the cold or just didn't care anymore."

Elkman looks back at the group of horses behind them as they lower their heads and graze on the sweet, long grasses. He waits awhile to hear if the rancher has more to say, before speaking.

"There are women that can make a go of it. Some just ain't cut from that hardy cloth. I was raised by one who could out-grit most any man. Ain't seen one in a spell, but they do appear in hard times."

Elkman glances over and tries to push the memories of Kent's sister from his head. James lets his eyes wander over the spread and pulls his Stetson hat down firm on his brow.

"I sure was looking forward to the boy coming up here to share this place with me. Didn't know if I could make him stick long but I was sure gonna try."

James looks over at Elkman and studies him a minute.

"Was his sister back from out East when you stopped?"

Elkman nods and flushes a bit. A twinkle sparks in the old rancher's eyes as the remembrances of the past experiences show on the younger cowboy's features.

"Now, she'll attract a decent man for that spread and I was hoping Kent would stick 'nd help me make a go of this place. There is something about a father and son that make it hard on landholdings. Here we could have been partners."

Elkman reminisces on his own childhood and spits away to the side. He wipes a finger across his mustache and stares over the wide expanse of valley.

"When you're working a hard-won spread, a good father and a good man ain't always the same thing to a boy."

James nods and gives his string of horses a tug.

"Let's bring 'em home and rustle up some grub."

They both look to the wood smoke trickling out of the stone chimney and their stomachs growl in a conversant unison. Elkman follows the rancher's lead as they travel the rim around the valley, riding at an easy lope.

Chapter 40

The rancher rides ahead in the lead toward the log structures of the ranch and Elkman follows behind. His gaze travels to a stand of trees near an overhanging outlook, and he veers toward the scenic view.

The horse stock trailing along, Elkman pauses near the rim of the bluff and looks down to stacks of sun-bleached buffalo bones piled below. He turns in the saddle and looks to the long, open approach to the buffalo jump and imagines the native population making use of the natural landscape in the hunt.

A low, rumbling grunt emanates from the nearby brush and a shock of anxiety shivers through the trailing horse stock. Elkman is spun further in the saddle as the fearful animals jerk the lead rope from his grip and flee away from the stand of trees and brush. Cursing under his breath, he watches as the mob of horse tails kick toward the other bunch not far ahead. His pack animal crowds close with ears pricked skyward as a low growl grumbles from concealment.

Elkman chokes up on his bridle reins and slowly backs his mount from the looming encounter. The pack animal spins, getting the lead rope tangled up under its tail, and instinctively kicks out with both hind legs. With a sharp jolt that takes a moment for the hurt to materialize, Elkman takes the full impact of the pack animal's hind hooves just above the knee. His horse stumbles back off kilter on the uneven footing before losing its balance and tumbling to the ground.

Pain throbs through Elkman's senses as his horse hits the terrain with a heavy thud, trapping his right leg and stirrup underneath. The pack animal continues to kick the lead rope from the tangle at its hind legs, and the capsized saddle mount holds the prone position on its side. Elkman grips the reins tight and keeps the horse's head turned away from the growling brush. The long equine legs kick out for terra firma, sending shudders of pain through the cowboy's trapped leg until the horse finally settles into submission.

Elkman tries to push himself from the pinned position under the saddle as the barrel-sized head of a grizzly bear rises from the scrubby bushes. The animal's long white choppers click menacingly as the grizzly licks his mouth of scrounged vegetation. The large head gives a shake and with a thrust of broad shoulders the bear rises to full height. The chest and arms of the long-haired beast stand above the sparse concealment, and the fur trembles as a guttural warning bellows forth.

The horizontal horse cranes its neck to see the looming predator and again kicks its legs and hooves to no effect. Elkman wraps his free hand around the butt of his rifle and tries to tug it from the pinned scabbard. He looks down to his exposed, swollen thigh and tries to restrain the horse from crushing his other limb.

The barrel of the rifle remains wedged between the ground, his leg, and the weight of the saddle animal. Elkman stares up at the grumbling grizzly bear. They match each other's gaze for a long moment, and Elkman stares into the dispassionate dark eyes of his potential death.

Flashes of living life's journey pass before Elkman in a brief encounter: his life on the farm, the war, traveling west, and then the never-ending journey of day-to-day survival. What seems like a stretch of minutes happens in a short, time-altering moment. The man and beast stare at another and wait for the fates of nature to decide.

A glimmer of satisfaction twinkles across the dark grizzly's gaze as it peers over a broad shoulder and drops to all fours. Elkman watches immobile as the burly animal mashes the foliage beneath and turns a massive head for one more peek at the vulnerable man and horse before it. The disinterested beast grunts a passive salute and ambles into the brush, disappearing into whence it came.

Suddenly aware of the pounding in his chest, Elkman hears the distant rumble of hooves as James and one of the ranch hands rides near. The extra hand rides bare-back on one of the mares and holds Elkman's pack animal in tow. With rifle in hand, the old rancher approaches and calls out.

"Eh, there fella . . . yer stock come in without ya so we come a searchin'."

Elkman holds back his tumbled mount and winces at the pain in both legs. The horses approach slowly and James steps down from the saddle to look over the situation.

"Hold'er there kid or that steed will roll the saddle o'er ya 'nd smash yer hip."

James takes a firm hold of the bridle and sets his rifle aside on the ground. He looks up at his ranch hand and then down at Elkman.

"How's yer other leg? It busted?"

"Don't feel that way, jest stuck. Hard to tell with all the pain in t'other."

The rancher looks over at Elkman's exposed leg, which has swelled the britches to a loaf-sized lump over the knee.

"What happened there?"

"Damned pack animal put two feet upside me and tumbled us to where we're at now."

The rancher looks up as his hired hand secures his horse and the pack animal to a nearby tree.

"I'm gonna guide yer horse to his feet and Jonas there will tug you free from gettin' rolled. You ready for it?"

"Ready as it's gonna get."

The ranch hand grips Elkman below the arms and plants his feet firmly. James gives a holler and pulls the horse's head skyward and away. As the horse rolls to gain footing, Elkman is pulled free while all parties move away to give the horse room to kick and maneuver to its feet. The saddle mount righted again, the horse rancher circles the animal, adjusts the saddle, and leads it a short distance to the other animals. He walks to where Elkman sits on the ground and kneels down.

"Yer horse seems fine enough. How are you?"

Elkman runs his hands gingerly down the length of his legs and feels for brokenness. "Nothing that won't heal."

"Ain't busted anything?"

"Not that I can tell."

James looks down at the bulge of swelling above the knee.

"Kin you walk on that?"

"Hell, I can ride if you get me up in the saddle."

They both laugh in pained relief.

"That may be, but you ain't riding far with it. Not to Virginia City in the next week I reckon."

Elkman struggles to his feet with the help of the ranch hand and hesitantly puts weight on the swollen leg.

"Damn, I'm not sure which leg hurts worse."

James shakes his head and grabs his rifle from the ground.

"Lookin' to me like you'll be lolling at my place a bit."

"Loafin' don't agree with me."

"You earned some time off and now you require it."

"I'd ruther help out in some way."

The rancher laughs, amused, and leads Elkman's horse nearer.

"Sure, I'll find work you can do from a rocker."

The two men help to hoist Elkman into the saddle and the leg-sore cowboy nearly passes out from the pain. Wincing and regaining his senses, Elkman looks down at James Mitchell.

"A little time out of the saddle could be good fer me."

Elkman lets his legs dangle as the old rancher walks the burdened mount toward his own and steps up into the slick-forked seat. The rancher looks back at the injured cowboy who leans down resting a hand on a swollen thigh and gives a fatherly nod. Elkman clings to the saddle and briefly looks back to where the grizzly disappeared into the brush. He closes his eyes a short moment and feels pangs of gratitude as he is led at a slow walk over the remaining distance to the ranch house.

Chapter 41

The bustling boomtown of Virginia City is full of life and the picture of a prospering western burg. The main street forms a sort of artificial canyon towering above with many two-story wood and brick buildings. His leg injury appearing recovered, Elkman rides along the street with his pack horse in tow and scans the dozens of unknown but familiar type faces. The commotion and mass activity of townspeople and commerce has a claustrophobic effect, putting Elkman ill at ease.

Near the end of the wide dirt main street, he veers off and stands his horse alongside a four-up hitched passenger mud-wagon. He looks beyond to the squat, brick structure marked Posting Office. He glances back up the thoroughfare again and steers his horse to the tying rail in front of the block building. Dismounting, he loops his reins over the wood rail and steps with a slight limp to the boardwalk. He watches the busy street another moment with distaste, then enters the stout jail-like posting agency.

Elkman steps inside and looks around the workspace filled with a clutter of packages and mail envelopes. He observes as the Post Attendant speaks with the Coach Driver and hands him several paper-bound parcels and a bundle of letters. The attendant peers over his small rimmed spectacles at Elkman as the coach driver moves past and exits to the outside.

"Can I help you, sir?"

"I'm supposed to receive a post from Cheyenne."

The man stares blank-faced. Elkman approaches the counter and the postman gets a quizzical expression.

"And . . . I'm supposed to guess whom it's for?"

Elkman follows the attendant's sarcastic gaze as his eyes travel over the dozens of packages and stacks of paper letters inside the cramped office.

"How would you do that?"

"I can't."

The two stare at each other a long moment then Elkman leans on the counter and looks behind at the vast bins of unsorted mail. "The name is T. H. Elkman."

Maneuvering his way around the clutter, the man thumbs through his register. He glances up at Elkman once and looks down again, placing his finger on an entry.

"Picked up a week ago."

"What do ya mean, picked up?"

The postman watches Elkman strangely for a moment and spins the ledger on its wire spine.

"Picked up by Tomas H. Elkman . . . . Signature, right here."

Elkman leans over and sees his name scribbled amongst dozens of others. He shakes his head as his temper rises.

"That son of a . . ."

Elkman turns on his boot heel, impulsively puts his hand to his holstered sidearm and marches stiff-legged to the door. The postal attendant clears his throat nervously and calls out.

"Excuse me? Is there a problem?"

The heavy wooden entry door swings open and Elkman turns and glares at all the freight items and mail stacked head-high in every corner of the room.

"Other than having 'nough of all this so called luxuries of civilization? Who are all these folks!"

The postman stares at the angry cowboy in the entryway inquisitively as Elkman lets the door slam behind him. Through the front iron-caged windows, past the stacks of parcels he watches Elkman slowly mount up, back his horses into the busy street, and ride away out of sight.

The postal attendant removes his glasses, wipes them on his necktie, and places them back on his nose. He looks around the cluttered room and shrugs. "Humph…"

The wide main street is tangled with wagons moving or hitched up and parked. Teams of horses and piles of merchandise ready for loading or delivery clog the throughways. Steering his horse around the chaos in his path then turning on a side avenue, Elkman fumes and cusses to himself. The mass of hectic individuals around him adds to his frustration as he maneuvers the busy crowded streets.

A man in a new suit of clothes dashes into the street cutting across Elkman's path, causing his horse to skitter sideways. Elkman spits his words angrily at the careless individual.

"Hell man! Watch where yer goin'."

The man looks up to apologize and surprise fills both their faces. "McGredy . . . ?"

The shocked gambler takes a measured step backward toward the boardwalk and smiles sheepishly.

"Tomas . . . how long you been in town?"

The expression on Elkman's face reveals the account as he puts a stern eye to McGredy's new outfit.

"Long 'nough . . . Nice new duds."

McGredy glances down at his new store bought outfit and brushes off faint dust smudges from travel along the street.

"Like 'em?"

Elkman puts his palm to the handle of his pistol and wraps his fingers around the wooden grip.

"Suit ya well enough to git buried in."

"Hold on now, I can explain."

"Ya best start, 'nd quick."

McGredy watches Elkman's temper flare and he takes another step back as he tugs on the bottom front of his vest. The horseback rider notices the gambler's lower vest pocket which usually lodges his gaming funds appears ample. McGredy instinctively pats the swelled pocket and grins unabashed. He peers over his shoulder with the fleeting thought to dash away while the flow of people continues all around them.

"Now, Tomas, you got no call to gun me down here in the street with all these nice people around . . ."

Elkman gives him a grave look.

"A thief don't deserve much better."

"Well, wait until I tell the story at least."

"I'm still listening 'nd ain't shot you yet."

McGredy halts his retreat and changes his defensive tactic as he steps up on the boardwalk. He throws the old familiar smirk toward Elkman and flashes him a wink. "You know how it is."

"I know how you are."

"See, I needed some money and it was all I could get my hands on. I've got that woman to impress and I couldn't show up in my trail clothes, could I? Besides, half of it was mine, right?"

Elkman relaxes the ready grip on his pistol and eases his horse away from the middle of the street.

"What happened to yer other earned money?"

"Well spent, well spent. Problem is, well . . . it barely got me across town."

Elkman sits atop his horse and looks down at McGredy. He sighs as he watches the big man stand against the flow of the crowded boardwalk.

"You damned fool."

McGredy smiles engagingly.

"Easy come, easy go, I say. Get yerself out of the street, hop down, and we'll go git ya your share."

Elkman moves his hand from his holstered pistol as McGredy's easy charm settles in.

"My share?"

"Of course. Step down and we'll git to it."

Elkman manuevers his horse to the hitching rail, gingerly climbs out of the saddle, and loops his reins on the crowded pole. He pulls his pack animal in from the street and ties him to the rail while peering from under his hat at McGredy.

"I'm a mite surprised you still have my funds still around. Ya didn't already find an investment for it?"

McGredy smiles and pulls his new pipe from his vest pocket along with a pouch of store-bought Tennessee tobacco from his coat.

"Hell, I wasn't going to spend yours . . . not for at least another day or so."

Chapter 42

The backside of town has more lascivious inclinations in its construction and the uncultured members of society occupying the street. McGredy in his new store-bought outfit looks slightly out of character among the pleasure-seeking laborers and cowhands. Elkman ambles with a slight limp alongside McGredy feeling more at ease amongst the frontier, rural type.

"Ya found that woman of yourn?"

McGredy pulls his pipe from his teeth and grins as he looks around cautious for watchful eyes upon him.

"Yeah, and if she sees me in this part of town there'll be hell to pay. She thinks these workin' type men are the source of 'nd a bad influence over my drinkin' 'nd gamblin' habits."

Elkman shrugs his shoulders and nods.

"Sounds like some good guidance for ya. What kind of woman is this? She ain't a whore is she?"

McGredy turns to face Elkman, surprise and shock in his expression.

"Jeez, Tomas, don't call her that! I know all types of females. Most of 'em is recreational sorts, but not all."

McGredy instinctively glances over his shoulder at a leisure-sale woman advertising her wares in the window. He smiles and tips his hat with respect.

"She sure ain't one to be seen on this particular street."

"Why she wasting her time with you?"

McGredy takes an empty puff of the darkened pipe and strikes a match on the porch support to light it again. He arches an eyebrow toward his old trail partner.

"Love is funny that way."

Elkman stops and appears astounded. He watches McGredy as a halo-ringed mist of tobacco smoke drifts from the bowl of the pipe over the unrepentant gambler.

"You in love?"

The large man beams and pulls on the lapels of his coat.

"No, but she is."

McGredy tips the back of his hat forward on his head, takes an exaggerated step forward and enters the carved wooden batwing doors of a saloon. Elkman lets the swinging doors flap a moment then follows McGredy inside.

Both men are bellied up to the bar with a bottle of whiskey, short glass tumblers, and a mug of beer each. Elkman and McGredy seem relaxed and content in the familiar surroundings. McGredy pours a round from the bottle and lifts his glass.

"Thanks for the drink, pard."

Elkman takes up his whiskey and clanks it on McGredy's tumbler. He swallows the hard liquor, snaps his glass down and winces with palms flexed on the stained wood surface. Elkman shakes it off, turns to lean his elbows back on the bar-top and studies the saloon's interior.

"So, you keep a place here?"

"Yep, a man's got to work."

McGredy pours another drink for them both. The big man sips on his then downs it with little more than a shiver. Elkman takes his beer mug in hand and gestures it toward the room.

"Don't suppose she knows 'bout it?"

"No need to bother a gal about the details. They don't care as long as ya got money in yer pockets. She's happy with knowin' that I get up most afternoons to make the rounds with customers."

"Customers?"

"Trade . . . My time at the cards for their money."

Elkman lifts his mug and takes a swallow. He observes, mildly surprised, as McGredy pours another whiskey and downs it.

"Who pays for yer drinks?"

"I get a lot of 'em comped since I do brisk business in here most evenings."

Elkman wipes his mustache and licks his lower lip as he speaks.

"It ain't honest work, but it is work."

"Hell, they water it down some anyway."

He watches as McGredy sets his empty glass on the bar and grabs up the whiskey bottle. The dark liquid swirls in the broken sunlight and Elkman smiles at ease.

"Good thing they do."

The sunlit bar room looks strangely odd and less appealing than it does in the dark of evening. Elkman takes up his glass of whiskey and sets the beer mug back on the bar top. Pouring another glassful for himself, McGredy raises it in a friendly toasting gesture.

"Well, here's to . . . trailing the journey north with the likes of me and yer still alive yet!"

Elkman lifts the contents in his glass.

"Despite yerself."

Smiling, they both down their drinks. McGredy pours them both another and rubs his close-cropped cheeks.

"What put the gimp in yer giddyup?"

"Had an encounter with nature and my packer kicked me above the knee on one side and the horse tumbled on my other."

McGredy shakes his head and grunts.

"Hell of a dangerous way to make a livin', relying on them four-legged beasts."

"I prefer it to yers."

McGredy opens his arms to the nearly empty saloon.

"I'd ruther deal with the dumb animals in here that are predictable and don't kick so hard."

He smiles and winks at Elkman.

"You gonna find a woman to cozy up to fer a bit 'nd enjoy the season? Miss Kay does have some pretty lady friends."

McGredy glances down at Elkman's dirt-worn clothes and muddy spur-strapped boots.

"You may have to use some of them earnin's to get yerself some fresh wardrobe 'for they let you in the parlor though."

Elkman looks out the front doors to the crowded street. His gaze seems to be filled with a lost and distant melancholy.

"This place ain't for me. I got a bit too much wander in my blood. A town gal seems the last thing I need involvin' with."

He downs his drink and McGredy casually pours him another.

"You goin' back to that ranch down south?"

Elkman swirls the dark colored liquid in his glass and responds quietly.

"Thought about it some."

He shakes his head and takes a sip.

"Maybe north a piece further or west through the mountains . . . away from all this."

McGredy nods and grabs up his beer mug from the bar. He takes a swallow from the mug and with both hands occupied, wipes his coat sleeve across his mouth.

"Too much for ya, eh?"

"I 'xpect so."

The well-dressed gambler grins and gives a slight gesture toward a working girl near a card game in the corner. Elkman notices McGredy's attention is pulled away and the chronic opportunist seems distracted as he watches the card players toss money to the center of the table.

"Know what yer sayin', Tomas. The rovin' itch'll surely hit me again when I least expect it or my luck wears thin 'round here."

McGredy finishes his beer and slides it back on the bar slab. Turning toward his former trail partner, McGredy pats his moneyed vest pocket.

"When you heading out?"

Elkman pours his remaining whiskey into his mug of beer and drinks it down in two large swallows. He rubs his middle section, contented, squeezes a hand on his sore thigh just above the knee, and looks to the empty doorway.

"'Bout now."

McGredy downs another dram of whiskey and places the cork back in the bottle. He tamps it down with his palm and slides it to the bartender with a wink. "Be right back."

He watches Elkman, amused, as the socially lubricated cowboy walks with a loose-hobbled gait toward the swinging doors and pushes through.

Elkman secures his supplies in a sailcloth sack over his pack animal and looks past his shoulder at McGredy watching.

"Don't you have some work to get to?"

McGredy smirks and glances over toward the door of the saloon.

"They'll be in there awhile passing their money around. Got to let 'em have a little fun 'fore giving it to me."

Elkman moves around his mount and raises his boot to the dangling stirrup. He takes a deep sobering breath and steps up into the saddle. McGredy walks forward and leans on the porch support post.

"You okay to ride?"

"I ain't got nowhere to be, so I won't be late."

"West, huh?"

"Yep, reckon so."

Tipping his hat back on his head, McGredy watches as Elkman gathers his reins and the lead rope to his pack animal.

"Good luck to ya then."

"You'll need it more."

"Yes, sir."

Elkman gives a final look down the street toward the booming town of Virginia City and its many growing structures and classes of people. His gaze rises past it all toward the lofty mountains in the distance. The lone horseback cowboy wheels his animals around and aims his trappings west. He taps his spurred heels and trots off through town toward the faraway high country.

McGredy knocks the dust off his boots on the adjacent porch post, looks up, and watches his friend depart. Alone on the boardwalk feeling a remote sense of loss, the solitary gambler stares as the image of the drifting cowboy slowly dissolves into the scenery by way of the crowd splitting, then covering back again.

The faraway peaks loom with a crown of snowy white on the horizon. A wandering cowboy with his finite belongings trails across lush pastures toward the high divide. The slow steady pace of man and horse puts an easy feeling to the cadence of life.

THE END

Afterword

Before the turn of the last century, I was a film studies student in Chicago completing one of my first Western film projects. The award-winning, 16mm short film *The Rustlers* was about two cowboys who stroll into a tough old west town to recover their lost stock.

With my cinematographer pal and classmate, Dan Farnam, and my friends in the acting troupe, *Kishwaukee Valley Vigilance Committee*, we were able to put together a cast of authentic cowboy characters. We even had a historic-looking town to use which was built on a friend's farm property . . . but what we didn't have was horses. As a Western filmmaker, I have since remedied the horse situation, but as a storyteller, I have never forgotten those cowboys who strolled into town with hard looks of determination, self-reliant grit, and guns at the ready.

Eric H. Heisner
January 22, 2016

T. H. Elkman

A Western novel by

Eric H. Heisner

www.leandogproductions.com